THUNDER OF WAR, LIGHTNING OF DESIRE:

Lesbian Historical Military Erotica

Edited by Sacchi Green

Thunder of War, Lightning of Desire
Edited by Sacchi Green

ISBN-13: 978-1-59021-592-0
ISBN-10: 1-59021-592-3

Edited by Sacchi Green
Cover art by Inkspiral Designs
Interior formatting by Kody Boye

Lethe Press, Inc.
118 Heritage Ave, Maple Shade, NJ 08052
lethepressbooks.com

TABLE OF CONTENTS

INTRODUCTION

FROM THE EDITOR, SACCHI GREEN

History, to my mind, is the greatest story ever told. As with any narrative constructed by humans, it has errors, omissions, and a fair share of outright fiction. History fascinates me as much as any intentional fiction, even though I've come to realize the ways in which the stories of certain populations were told, and were not told. Women have been largely ignored by preponderantly male historians, and LGBT people were either ignored or vilified, but in recent years more and more has come to light about their lives and roles, even in warfare, that most dramatic, memorable, and endlessly rehashed area of history.

This book is admittedly fiction. These are stories of lesbians who are active participants in warfare, and stories of lesbian sex as well, with passionate characters finding each other amidst the storm of war. Women come together for comfort, for relief, driven by adrenaline and hormones, hurling their pleasure into the teeth of mortality and cultural oppression. They share frantic embraces, dark humor, or whatever it takes to get them through the night, and through the war. Tender or raw, harsh or healing, always intense, the sex is as integral to each story as any other component, including the historical settings.

While the characters and some of the events are fictional, the settings are essentially authentic. There could be endless such stories told, beginning even before what we think of as recorded history. What might Artemis the Huntress with her bow or Athena Promachos with her spear and armor (both traditionally virgins, however that might be interpreted), tell us about the unrecorded cultural roles of even earlier generations of women? And what about legends of Amazons, and recent discoveries of ancient graves where certain women were buried along with weapons of war in the same way as men?

For this book, though, we chose to focus our attention on more recent history, from about 1860 to 1970, a span of only 110 years, but years of tremendous change, upheaval, and influence on the world we know now.

We begin, of course, with the American Civil War. Research has shown that more than six hundred women—probably many more—passed as men to fight in this war, and that's not counting the nurses and spies. We can only speculate as to how many of them may have been lesbians (a term not then in use), but among women with the daring and strength to flout cultural norms and put their lives on the line, the percentage was most likely higher than in the population as a whole. There certainly were some. The boyish Confederate soldier of Pascal Scott's "War of the Rebellion," endearingly awkward in a first adventure with both a girl and a mail-order "manhood," is entirely plausible, and so is the strong minded runaway slave serving with a Union regiment in Victoria Janssen's "Found."

Set more than three decades later, with a shift in mood and atmosphere, we have the story of an uprising far away in China, The Boxer Rebellion of 1900. In J.B. Hickok's "Forbidden Love" an anti-Western-Imperialism mob (backed by the Empress Dowager) forces Europeans and Chinese Christians to barricade themselves in the Legation Quarter of Beijing, and a British army nurse caught up in the furor becomes entangled in political upheaval within the Forbidden City as she tries to heal a desperately ill Royal Concubine. A decade and a half later, in World War I (The Great War, aka The War to End Wars), women served as ambulance drivers as well as nurses. In Victoria Janssen's "Delivery" a British woman whose company manufactures field telephones gets unexpected transport in an ambulance, and a transformative connection with an Arizona cowgirl volunteering as a driver.

In Jessica Taylor's "Eagle of Death, Raven of War," set at about the same time in Russia, a young recruit with Maria Bochkareva's Women's Battalion of Death finds her smoldering hero worship flaring into much more as they brace to charge the German trenches.

Not all conflicts pitted nation against nation. Soon after WWI, in 1921, the United States saw its largest armed rebellion since the Civil War, when miners fighting to unionize in West Virginia bravely faced local, state, and even U.S. Army forces and bombings by U.S. Government planes. Some strong women worked in those mines, alongside what men were left after WWI, and in "The Battle of Blair Mountain" Dena Hankins shows us two unforgettable characters, mountain-wise and gun-savvy, taking what scant cover they can find from the bombing, and what fierce distraction they can find with each other.

Then another two decades, and, inevitably, another war, World War II, spreads across continents and seas. Cara Patterson, in "The Girl in the Window," shows a Russian woman sniper on duty in the ever-shifting rubble of Stalingrad, and an eerily attractive girl who has her own personal ways of killing enemies. In stark contrast, on the other side of the world, Jove Belle's American WACs in the South Pacific are stuck against their wills on an island well behind the front lines, where boredom might kill them if they didn't have each other to explore in "Moments of Peace."

Another decade. Another war. Nurses in a MASH unit in Korea have no time for boredom, or for anything beyond using all their skill and energy treating massive wounds and eluding enemy shelling, but in "Watching," by CB Potts, lust finds a way, between emergency surgery and loading patients on helicopters and pulling up stakes to move the camp.

Yet another decade, and...well, you know the drill by now. Vietnam. My own story "Danger" takes a somewhat difference tack, with flashbacks to the still-raging war in Vietnam, but also with hints of the lingering effects of war on those who've returned. An Army nurse rotated back to duty at Walter Reed Hospital and an AWOL ambulance driver meet in the turmoil of a new kind of battle, in Greenwich Village, New York City, on June 28th, 1969. You've heard of the Stonewall Inn? This piece felt strange to write, because I knew the times and the territory myself. I wasn't there on that day, or days, but I'd been there before, and was there many times afterward. It's unsettling to think of one's own life as history. History, though, is endless, as far as our minds can comprehend, and all our stories, all our lives, are ongoing parts of it whether recorded or not.

Nothing I've told you here does justice to the full sweep and complexity of the stories in this book, or the talents of the writers. There are many more stories from this period equally worth telling. Try researching the Dahomey Amazons fighting the French in Africa in the 1890s, for instance, or women working undercover for Irish Independence in the 1920s, or the Russian Night Witches of WWII flying bombers—clumsy biplanes left over from that Great War that didn't end war after all—to harry the German Army, or Israeli women with the Haganah organization fighting for statehood for decades. The list goes on and on.

If history interests you as much as it does me, you probably know all this already, and if you don't, exploring any of these would be well worth your while. Unless you have the great good fortune to come across some especially revealing memoirs or letters, though—and please let me know if you do—you'll need to rely on your own imagination for the sex behind the warfare. I hope you're as glad as I am that the writers of the stories told here have already done that for you, and done it so scorchingly well.

Sacchi Green
Amherst, MA

WAR OF THE REBELLION

BY PASCAL SCOTT

1862: The War Between the States: Tennessee

> Rebellion: from the Latin, rebelliō. Resistance to or defiance of any authority, control or tradition

"Mackey, my skeesicks, what yer a'needin' is some horizontal refreshments. Hogmagundy. In plainer words, Mackey boy, you need to ride a Dutch gal." This is my tentmate, Jacob Allen Carpenter, speaking. Like me, Carpenter's a private newly enlisted in the 58th Infantry North Carolina. "You know what they say," Carp muses. "All shit and no sugar makes Mack a dull boy."

For the last six months, Carp and I have shared a tent here at Camp Johnston, Tennessee, where we've been sent for maneuvers. Inside our diggings—six by eight by six feet in size—there's room for a folding chair, a small table, and two narrow beds. Except for us and the occasional visitor, there's not room for much else. Last summer, we were marched to Camp Johnston to learn how to be Confederate soldiers—how to follow an order, fire a Springfield rifle, and forage for blackberries if need be. When the Army thinks we're ready, we'll be moving out for battle. Until then it's drill-drill-drill, all the day long.

Before he was a soldier, Carpenter was a farmer. Back in Burke County where he's from, Carp's got a girl, he tells me. They've "done the dance," and he's promised to marry her when the War is over. "But that don't mean I can't enjoy the ladies in the meantime," he says. Carp's got big ears that stick out to the sides of his head and a big mouth that works quicker than his brain. By ladies, Carp is referring to the girls who come to the camp most evenings to share a good time with anyone who's got a few extra greybacks. On those nights, when the tent is occupied by Carp and his companion, I sit outside on a tree stump, filling my pipe with the sweet Durham tobacco that comes with our rations.

"Lookee here, Mackey" Carp is saying. He comes over to the bed where I'm lying, trying to rest after the day's drills. He tosses something onto my chest, and it lands with a plop. I pick it up and read, "G.S. Hoskins and Company." Carp explains that it's a catalogue of merchandise from a warehouse in Richmond, Virginia. His sticky fingers turn the pages until they find their destination. He points. "Read this, Mackey." I read silently. "No, no, Mackey, read it out loud so's I can hear it." Carp reads only a little and has trouble with many words. I read aloud:

"Available for purchase by discerning gentlemen. Now in stock: stereoscopic pictures from Paris, France showing two or more figures, photographed from life, engaged in sexual enjoyment. Yours for $9 per dozen. Or for only $3 per dozen, postpaid, *cartes de visite* of Paris and London voluptuaries portraying the mysteries and delights of naked female beauty, male and female together, and separate."

"Got me some of them pictures," Carp tells me. "They're real fine. I'll show 'em to ya later. Go on." I continue:

"For your reading pleasure, choose from among our many titles: Fanny Hill, Confessions of a Lady's Waiting Maid, The French Courtesan, Venus in the Cloister, The Marriage Bed, Secret Passions, Physiology of Love, Prostitution in Paris, Maria Monk, Memoirs of a Man of Pleasure. Also available: three kinds of condoms (both skin and India rubber) including Dr. Powers' French Preventatives and Goodyear

Rubber Goods. Love powders, French ticklers, dildos..."

"Got me one of them French ticklers, too. Makes the gals crazy."

I'm embarrassed, but I have to ask. "What's a French tickler?"

"Ah, Mackey my hobbadehoy. Yer a virgin, ain't ya?"

He doesn't wait for an answer.

"It's what they call a condom with some added features. You put it on your pole before you give the gal a poke."

"Oh," I say. "What's a dildo?"

He turns the pages again until he finds the one he wants. "Lookee here, Mackey. *That*'s a dildo."

I can feel my eyes widen. What I'm looking at is a drawing of something that looks like a man's penis inserted through something that looks like a harness. There are loops in the harness—or maybe they're straps, I can't tell—and the contraption seems to be sewn together out of some kind of hospital cloth. I feel my head tilt and my eyebrows knit together. Carp notices.

"Doncha fret about that, Mackey boy. Some sawbones came up with the idea for the unfortunate lads who'd got their cock-an'-tallywags blowed off."

I blush, not at his words but at an idea starting in my head. Nobody, not even Carp, knows my secret, that the only thing I'm missing is my manhood, and now right in front of me in black and white, here it is. Available by mail from G.S. Hoskins and Company for $15—a lot of money by anybody's reckoning. But with my bounty and my monthly pay of $11, I have it in hand. I determine to write to Hoskins straight away.

"Mackey, my virgin lad," Carp is saying. "Yer needin' to put yer cock in the cock pit. Yer finger into mary jane. Yer johnson in the doodlesack. Er ya gettin' my drift, Mackey boy? We gotta get you a fancy girl. In the meantime, though, lemme show you them pictures."

By now you may be wondering how I happened to arrive at this station in life. I'll tell you what I told the Recruiting Officer in Mitchell County: My name is John Albert McAfee, and I hail from Caldwell County, North Carolina. I am eighteen years of age last April, and I'm free from bodily defect and mental infirmity (far as anyone can tell). When my old Sharp's rifle is aimed true, I can hit a squirrel at sixty yards. I'm strong and sober and fit for service. And after what the Bluebellies did to my brother, I'm wantin' to kill me some Yankees.

That's what I told him. His eyes—Carolina blue like mine—lit up with interest, and he asked why a young lad like me was enlisting so far from home. I must have heard about the Caldwell Rough and Ready Boys, and why wasn't I signing up with them? I thought he might ask and had my answer prepared.

"My ma don't know, sir," I said. "It would kill her if she thought she might lose another son. You see, she's already lost one boy to the War. My brother, Abram Knox McAfee."

He frowned, and his forehead wrinkled with straw-colored lines. I wondered if I'd made a mistake. Did the Army have some rule I didn't know about? Something that would stop a boy from enlisting if his family had already suffered a casualty? I tried to remember the boys from Caldwell County who had died in this war: John Marley, George Friddle, James Parleir, Eli Bower. The brothers Genison and Absalom Caudle, both gone now.

"I'm sorry about your brother," the Recruiter said and sighed. "And I'm sorry you feel that way about the Yanks. I'm afraid you'll discover in time that they are men, too, with brothers and mothers just like you."

I didn't know quite what to make of this information, so I held my tongue.

"Show me your hands," he commanded.

I lay my hands, palms up, on the table between us. My hands are large for a girl's and calloused.

"Now your teeth," he said. I hesitated for a moment. My teeth? I pulled up my gums with my fingers, snarling like a dog. He peered into my mouth with a satisfied expression.

"Good," he said. "I am pleased to inform you that you have passed your physical exam. The Army requires that you have a finger for pulling a trigger and enough teeth to open a can of gun powder. I hereby witness that you have both."

He finished filling in the blank spaces on an official-looking form, signed it with a flourish, and turned it upside down so I could read it.

I, John Albert MacAfee, born in Caldwell County in the State of North Carolina aged 18 years and by occupation a farmer do hereby acknowledge to have voluntarily enlisted this 24th day of July 1862 as a Soldier in the Army of the Confederate States of America to serve for the period of the War, unless sooner discharged by proper authority...

He pointed to a line near the bottom and gave me the steel nib pen. "There," he said, tapping the place. "Ya know how to write?"

"Yes, sir," I said. "My ma saw to that."

I signed: John Albert MacAfee.

"Welcome to this man's army, Private MacAfee," the Recruiter said.

It was done.

Here's what I didn't tell him. My real name is Pauline Sarah McAfee, and I was born every bit a female person. John Albert McAfee was my baby brother who died when he was just a wee babe sucking at my mama's tit. Now, it *is* true that Ma didn't know I was enlisting, although she'd learn soon enough, when I wrote to tell her. But that's not the reason I walked most of a day to Mecklenburg County to join the Confederate Army. Everyone in Caldwell County knows the McAfees, and they know that John Albert McAfee died a long time ago and is buried in our little cemetery on the farm.

The McAfee Farm—you may have heard of it—is down by the Catawba River on good fertile bottomland. We've been in these foothills more than 100 years now. My great-great-granddaddy arrived way back in 1751, after *The Shirley*, sailing from Rotterdam by way of Orkney in Scotland, docked in Philadelphia. (I've heard the tale seems like a thousand times). He and my great-great-grandma made the rough ride down the Old Wagon Trail until they got to the mountains of North Carolina. They'd been told a lot of their kinfolk were here, and they were right: by that time the Scots-Irish had chased out the Cherokee and claimed this region as their own.

I could tell you more: how when the Revolution came, Albert McAfee made bootlegged whiskey for the troops. How Ma always thought that should qualify her to be a Daughter of the Revolution (the snooty members of that ladies' club disagreed). But that, as Ma says, would be more than you need to know.

Now, hold on there just one darn minute, I know you're thinking. But you're a *girl*. You can't just up and join the CSA. And you're right. It took a bit of subterfuge on my part to do what I've done. (My word for today, and don't feel bad if you need to look it up. Ma taught us to "increase your vocabulary" by one word each day—she was a teacher before she married my daddy—through reading, mostly, but also by listening to educated people when they speak. Ma taught us children to "respect Mr. Webster." *Subter-fuge, from the Latin* subter—*below—and* fugere—*to flee. Meaning: that to which one resorts to for escape or concealment.* Once you get the hang of them, words are pretty easy).

My subterfuge involved the hiding of my gender. In my case it wasn't all that hard. At five feet six inches I'm tall for a girl and not all that pretty (truth be told). I have nice features, people say, especially my eyes, which show everything I'm feeling if I'm not careful. I'm flat as a pancake across the chest, with not much of a rear end, either. Every spring, when I take the wagon to Charlotte for supplies, with my big shirt and baggy britches and my hair up under my cap, I'm mistaken for a boy until I speak, and then folks get embarrassed and can't apologize quick enough.

You may be wondering what my daddy had to say about all this. The fact is he had nothing to say. You see, Daddy died of Influenza long before the War of Northern Aggression began, and he's buried back there in the McAfee Cemetery right next to John Albert. Ma's been raising us—A.K. and me and the youngest, Elizabeth Amanda—all by herself. It's been hard on her, but she never complained, that is until we lost A.K.

Ma kept the last letter he wrote to her, postmarked Virginia, and she's read it a hundred times:

Dear Ma,

I hasten to let you know I am still alive. We have been fighting fifteen days and we have lost thirty-two men out of the company, four wounded, twenty-eight prisoners. I have just got off the battle field and I don't think I ever saw as many dead Yankees in my life. I think that they have lost ten to one. All of the Caldwell boys were taken prisoner but me and the Captain and First Lieutenant. We were wounded and I am so near worn out that I can't write. So you can understand. I have captured a heap of Yankees. I wish that you had them. You must excuse the bad letter. I will write when I can. No more for this time.

Your son,

A.K.

That was the last we heard, and then sometime later there was a letter from Colonel James Johnston Pettigrew saying he regretted to inform us that Private Abram Knox McAfee had been mortally wounded in battle. That was the first time I'd ever heard Ma swear. "Damn Yankees," she said, before she started crying. "Damn them all to hell." That's when I knew what I had to do.

First thing the CSA gave me was a thin, new hundred dollar bill—my enlistment bounty. A bare-breasted lady was on the front; I flipped her over, half expecting to see a bare-assed woman on the back (instead, there was nothing at all). Backside or no backside, I was more than happy to have her. Next thing I got was my uniform. The Quartermaster watched as I changed out of my dusty traveling clothes, so I turned my own backside to him, knowing he couldn't tell a thing about my sex based on that view. I decided right then and there that for the length of my stay in the Army I would feign modesty. I'd be one of those bashful boys too shy to show his private parts. *(Word for today: feign. From the Latin* feindre, *to invent. Meaning: to pretend, to represent by a false appearance of.)*

When I was dressed, in my loose-fitting trousers and my jacket buttoned up to my chin (to hide my lack of an Adam's apple), with brogans on my feet and a kepi on my short-clipped head of hair, the Quartermaster took me aside and looked me up and down. Then he bent so near that I could smell the tobacco on his breath. "I think yer keepin' a secret, son," he said.

I got real nervous then, but I tried my best not show it. I lowered my voice, as I was starting to do now by habit.

"What do you mean, sir?" I said.

"Yer no eighteen years of age. Yer just a boy. What are ya? Fourteen? Fifteen maybe? Ya ain't even got a beard yet."

Relief washed over me like an Appalachian rain. "Ya got me, sir," I said. "But please. Promise me you won't tell. I want to fight the Yankees."

"Good boy," he said and winked. "Ain't none-a-my beeswax is how I see it."

Ragged out in our new uniforms we looked as gay as you please, the boys of the 58th Infantry and me, gay enough for girls to notice as we marched past—waving their white hankies at us like so many flags of support. We waved back at them all and grinned and flirted, kicking up the rutted, dirt streets of Marion and Asheville and Mars Hill, on our way to Camp Johnston, Tennessee.

Word for today: dildo. From the Italian diletto, a lady's delight; origin Greek olisbos. Meaning: an implement resembling the male member for which it is said to be a substitute. Also known as a mandrake, godemiche, the widow's comforter, the little soldier, laughy taffy, my secret friend.

It arrives with autumn in a plain brown wrapper. I hide it from Carp and unwrap it when he's gone out with his possums to scrounge up some bark juice. I've thought to order a few books, just in case he wonders why I'm buying merchandise from G.S. Hoskins. I leave those on my bed where he can see them, wrap the dildo and harness in a dishcloth, and hide it inside my haversack.

"Heard you got somethin' in the post," Carp says when he comes in. From his breath, I assume he was successful in his search for red eye. I show him the titles: *Memoirs of Fanny Hill*, *Confessions of a Lady's Waiting Maid*, and *The French Courtesan*. The books are small enough to fit into a soldier's pocket and bound in dark cloth. They could be little Bibles for all anybody could tell. Carp picks up *Fanny Hill* and leafs through it.

"No pictures," he says.

I open to the first page and begin reading aloud:

Letter the First. Madam, I sit down to give you an undeniable proof of my considering your desires as indispensible orders. Ungracious then as the task may be, I shall recall to view those scandalous stages of my life, out of which I emerged, at length, to the enjoyment of every blessing in love...

Carpenter lies on his bed and listens. After awhile I hear him snoring. I blow out the candle lantern that sits on the table between our beds. I pull my haversack closer to where I'm perched on the edge of the hay-stuffed bed sack. In the dark, I reach inside the pack until I find the cloth covering the dildo. I unwrap it and touch my new purchase. It's made of rubber and feels hard and pliant at the same time. It feels long and thick. At the base there's a molded piece a little bigger than the cup of my hand.

I finger the straps, feel how they tie and adjust. I pull the harness over my feet, my legs, and up until it hugs the fork of my body. I adjust the straps until they're tight. I stand. It's heavier than I'd imagined. I hold it, stroke it a little, getting used to the sensation, the feeling of having a cock and balls. I like it. Silently, I loosen the harness and return the dildo to its hiding place in my haversack. My secret friend.

She tells me her name is Belle and says she's a gift from Private Carpenter. She's pretty, I think, with eyes the color of hazelnuts and lips that are full, rubbed red. Her hair is dark brown, almost black, parted down the middle in a neat line and pulled back in a braid. She seems young, maybe fifteen or sixteen. She avoids my stare.

"Belle?" I say.

"Belle," she repeats. "It's French. It means beautiful."

"Then it's an apt name," I say. "Are you French? By blood, I mean."

"No," she says. "Well, yeah, a lit'l. Ma says we got a drop of French blood in us. Jus' a drop."

"Then that's all you need," I say.

She shrugs. "I guess. I'd like to see Paris someday. Paris seems so—I dunno—romantic."

"I'd take you to Paris," I say. She looks directly into my eyes for the first time. I don't know what she sees there but in her eyes I read doubt followed by a quick flash of hope, then sadness. "Sure you would, soldier boy," she says.

Carp has paid Belle her fee of three dollars for the evening and left us alone in our tent. I don't know what he's told her, but I imagine that the subject of my virginity has been discussed. Belle takes a few steps toward the table where a candle is burning inside a wood-and-glass lantern. She bends slightly and blows it out. The only light left is the moon, bright and full tonight. Moonlight filters through the canvas walls and as my eyes adjust, I see her in silhouette, the line of her arms lifting her plaid dress over her head, followed by her chemise. She undoes her braid, shakes out her hair, lets it fall in dark waves.

I pull off my trousers and top-shirt until I'm down to my undershirt and drawers. She takes my hand and gently pushes me onto the bed. She lies on top of me for a moment and then rolls onto her back at the same time that she pulls me on top of her. She kisses me then—my first kiss from a girl—and her lips taste as sweet as rock candy. I breathe in the scent of her skin; it smells like rain and the earth back home in spring. Her lips are soft. They part and something darts into my mouth, licks my teeth.

"You really are green," she says. "Gimme your tongue."

I stick my tongue into her mouth and her tongue meets mine, tips it, teases it. Something between my legs warms with pleasure. She opens her legs then and pulls me closer. Carp has told me what to do and shown me pictures, and I try now to remember. I pull the dildo out of my drawers and lay it between her thighs. She sucks in a little breath and her stomach flattens. I push the cock closer. It bumps up against her pelvic bone and doesn't go in. I push harder and before I can stop her, her hand is down, reaching for it. When she finds it, she freezes. Her breath catches and I wonder if she knows. Can she tell? Does a rubber dildo feel anything like a flesh-and-blood cock? All this happens in an instant. Before I can finish the thought, she has pulled the head inside. She pushes herself down on me, and I am closer than I've ever been to another human being.

I balance myself over her, my hands flat on the bed sack. I can feel her breasts pushing up against my shirt, her nipples erect, her belly rising to meet me as I thrust. And she's thrusting back, arching her back. She's moaning now, and it's suddenly easier, I'm slipping in and out inside her, going deeper and deeper, our bodies making slapping sounds against each other. I hear her breathing: short, hard breaths, and I swear I can hear my own heart beating like mad. She grabs my hair and pulls my face down over her face, and her eyes open wide, catching the moonlight.

"Yes," she moans. "Yes, yes..."

I find a rougher rhythm and push into her deeper still. The base of the dildo is cuffing the warm spot between my thighs, and she's trembling, and her trembling reaches into me. I take her trembling and meet it with my own trembling body until I lose myself and crash into her as I hear her cry out. She lifts up and bucks and wraps her legs around me so tightly I think I might break.

Then she falls away, limp and spent. I roll off and arrange my cock back inside my drawers. I look at her face. It's wet with sweat, glistening in the moonlight. Her eyes are closed.

"Marry me, Belle," I say. She opens her eyes.

"What?" she says.

"I said, 'Marry me.'"

I think I see the corners of her mouth start upward, daring a smile. "Why would ya wanna marry *me*?"

Before I can answer she's up, off the bed. She pulls her chemise over her head. Next comes the dress. Her arms are long like her legs and lovely.

"What did you say your name was?"

"McAfee," I tell her. "John Albert McAfee. They call me Mackey."

"Mackey," she repeats. "You're sweet, Mackey. I hope we can do this again."

She pauses. "You're different, ya know," she says. "You're not like the other boys, are you?"

I don't know how to answer this. She seems to be considering something, and I'm thinking, does she know? And, if she knows, will she give me away?

"Emily," she says at last.

"What?" I say.

"My name. It's not really Belle. That's just what I tell my, ah, gentlemen. My name is Emily."

"Emily," I repeat. I say it again, more softly this time and in something closer to my own voice. "Emily."

We have two more nights together, Emily and me, before the 58th gets deployed to the Cumberland Gap. We're told only that the Army of East Tennessee needs our support. Carp slaps me on the back in anticipation. "Mackey, ya ole' fucker, we gonna kill us some Yanks!"

Emily stays behind in Johnston Depot. I ask her to wait for me, and she laughs and calls me a silly boy. I say, "Promise me, Emily. Promise me you'll be here when I come back for you." Somewhere a mountain moves when she says, "I promise you, Private John Albert McAfee. I'll be here when you come back for me."

I could tell you more: how we fought at Cumberland for forty-eight long hours and how Carp was wounded and captured and shipped to Camp Douglas, the Godawful Union prison in Chicago, where he survived the smallpox outbreak only to die of pneumonia in the winter of '63.

I could tell you how I killed a Yank at Chickamauga and how

when I looked down at his corpse, I saw that he was a boy no older than me, lying dead with his dark curls scattered around his face. I could tell you that he was dressed in uniform—blue and garnished with gold braid—and that his uniform seemed to tell the story of a loving mother who had sent her boy off to the killing fields of war. I could tell you that his cap had fallen beside him and bore the number of a New York regiment. I could tell you that standing over the boy whose life I had ended, I was sick to my heart at what I'd done.

And I could tell you how in the spring of 1864, Private John Albert McAfee deserted the Confederate States Army, how he left his gray uniform folded foursquare in a pile in his tent. And how Pauline Sarah McAfee borrowed a dress from Emily Ann Copenny to disguise herself as a girl, and how Miz McAfee and Miz Copenny were last seen leaving Tennessee together on a train headed south.

I could tell you what the rumors say now that the War is over, that there are two women living in the French Quarter of New Orleans, residing discreetly as man and wife. I could tell you about that and about so many other things, about war and rebellion and death and life and love. I could tell you all that and more but if I did, it would surely fill a book.

FOUND

BY VICTORIA JANSSEN

1863: The War Between the States: Virginia

The bare trees left her too exposed, so Clodia hid herself in the heavy, scratchy underbrush, a rabbit gone to ground.

Dusk fell, and with it the temperature. Clodia dragged over such branches and leaves as she could reach, making a sort of blanket to cover the torn remnants of her bodice. She pulled her petticoats in as tightly as she could manage, burrowing her feet under a litter of dead leaves and dry pine needles. Her bare toes were too cold to detect if insects or centipedes took refuge there as well, and for that she was grateful. She had learned, in recent days, to cling to such small mercies, because she couldn't grasp much beyond the present moment. Over and over she had reminded herself that she was free now, but she hadn't been able to truly believe that, not down in her bones, not when she lived with a constant terror of capture and retribution.

She closed her eyes, trying not to think of how her shivering intensified the soreness of her muscles, and how her stomach cramped with hunger. There wasn't much to scavenge in the winter. Crackling leaves clung to her fraying braids and scraped against her bruised face. She couldn't muster the energy to reach out of her nest to remove them. In the distance, she could hear sporadic gunfire, reminder of her peril.

Perhaps the soldiers would not come closer. Perhaps they would. What would she do if they found her? If the soldiers were from the North, she might survive; depending on the sort of men they were, they might or might not rape her, but she thought they would be less likely than their enemies to kill her outright or deliver her to a worse fate. She might be able to offer local knowledge in exchange for safety or at least for some food. If the soldiers were from the South, their response would depend on whether she was seen as valuable property, or not; also on whether she was recognized, and if her crime had come to light.

If soldiers came, it would be best to run.

Clodia couldn't even imagine herself running just now, or even walking another step. Would she really care if she fell asleep and never woke? What did she have to live for, without Diana? She was so exhausted she could not even muster hope of the sun rising tomorrow.

The gunfire slowed, then died away. Too cold to sleep, she shivered into an uneasy sort of dozing trance, welcoming the transient numbness of body and mind it brought.

"Get up."

The voice was harsh, as if scraped raw. Something poked into Clodia's bruised side and she gasped, curling around the pain. At least it distracted from her terror at being found.

"Hey, gentle, now," a deeper male voice said. Tears pricked her eyes at the barest hint of kindness she heard, and she opened her eyes, clumsily trying to sit up and ruthlessly crushing the faint hope she felt.

Two soldiers towered above her. Their uniforms were dark blue, Union uniforms, spattered to the knee with reddish mud. Her gaze traveled higher and she sucked in a startled breath. Their hands were dark-skinned. She looked higher and confirmed that the two men were black. Except one of them, though dressed in a man's uniform, was not a man at all, and Clodia knew her. Was she dreaming?

Diana was the only woman Clodia had ever imagined she could call friend, at least until the day their owner had left Diana bloodied on the ground and taken Clodia into the cottage where he kept his mistress. Clodia hadn't escaped that one-roomed building until three days ago.

Diana had fled the plantation shortly after war broke out;

Clodia had feared her dead and mourned her in the depths of the night, though she knew Diana had likely never forgiven her for giving in, for choosing further subjugation over death. Now here Diana stood, her sturdy form armored in dark blue wool, a brimmed cap pulled low over her cropped hair, a carbine slung casually over one arm.

Clodia stared. She had to be hallucinating. Or simply mistaken.

The male soldier reached out a hand. "Let me help you up, ma'am." He had a quick, crisp accent, and she realized he was probably a free man, from the Northern states. She had never seen a free black person before. He didn't look all that different. He said, "Can we help you?"

Diana took a step back, her carbine at the ready; he glanced at her and said, chidingly, "Daniel, she's just a slip of a thing."

"Might be a spy," Diana—Daniel—said, gruffly.

There was no point in denial just now. Clodia staggered as she stood, as if all her blood had rushed to her feet. She leaned heavily against the soldier's arm for a moment, recovering her balance while he spoke rapidly, persuasively. Slowly, things came back into focus.

She looked at the men again. Daniel's expression held significance, warning. Communication. Clodia wasn't dreaming. Daniel was Diana, hair cropped, face less pinched, but still Diana.

"I'm not a spy," she said, working to articulate the words around her swollen lip and bruised jaw. She stared Diana in the eye, but the only word she could muster was "Please."

Diana glared at her for a moment, then turned to her companion. "What are we supposed to do with her, Joseph? She'll only slow us down."

"We sure as hell can't leave her here," Joseph stated. "What's your name, miss?"

Was Diana angry at her? At something else? Long experience at keeping her curiosity close prevented her from asking. "My name's Clodia," she said. "Don't send me back. Please."

"We won't do that," he said. "You're safe now."

Diana rolled her eyes. "None of us are safe, we're scarce a mile from the lines. Joseph, you can drag her along if you like, but I'm going to make sure nobody gets the drop on us between here and camp." And with that, she strode forward without waiting for them to follow.

Clodia disentangled her arm from Joseph's. "I can walk," she insisted. "I'll make myself useful at the camp. I can cook, and—"

Joseph held up a hand. "No need to convince me, miss. I can see you've had a rough time of it, and our camp's location isn't much of a secret right now, what with all the shooting going on. You just let me know if you need my arm."

Clodia didn't see Diana again until that evening, at the Union camp. Upon arrival, she'd swiftly been surrounded by dark-skinned soldiers, who'd overwhelmed her with offers of rations and blankets. It had been difficult to keep her composure; there were so many of them, and they crowded close; it didn't matter that their intentions were good. Shortly after that, she'd been questioned at length by a trio of white officers. She'd given them as much information as she could about the local terrain and the nearby plantations, but since this was the farthest she'd ever traveled, her knowledge was limited. Luckily, all she told them fit with information they already possessed, reassuring them that she wasn't a spy for the Confederacy. Apart from that, they didn't appear all that interested in her, which was a relief.

At last, she was released into Joseph's custody. No longer carrying a carbine, he waited outside, Diana at his side, her expression unreadable. He said, "The laundresses are putting together some clothing for you."

Clodia clutched her blanket more closely around herself. "Thank you."

Diana said, "You can go on to supper, Joe. I'll take care of her from here."

Joseph looked surprised, but left them with a friendly salute. Diana said, in a low voice, "You didn't say nothing. About me."

Clodia shook her head. "I wouldn't. They don't—"

"No, they don't know what I am. If they did, they'd send me home right quick."

"I wouldn't tell," Clodia repeated. She tried to think what else to say. No more words came. She'd eaten, but lack of sleep left her distant and almost dizzy, and her side was stiff and sore.

Diana looked immensely relieved. "Come on, then," she said. "I'll clean up those cuts of yours."

Clodia had expected to be stared at as they traversed the muddy paths between tents. However, she received only a few brief glances before the men returned to studiously cleaning rifles, cooking over campfires, and playing cards. They were all white men, at least until they reached the outskirts of the camp, the last group of tents before the animal pickets and wagons. She could see a few women, all white, moving among the wagons, carrying loads of laundry, and one arm-in-arm with a soldier, both of them singing lustily and drunkenly.

"Don't go over there," Diana said, taking Clodia's arm to lead her in another direction. To Clodia's surprise, Diana had a tent to herself, though it wasn't roomy. "Marcus and Pompey died of the typhoid," she explained, as the tent flap fell closed behind them. "Sit."

Clodia's legs willingly collapsed beneath her. "Thank you," she said. "I don't know what I would have done."

Diana knelt, holding a jug of water and some rags. "Stayed alive somehow," she said. "You're good at that." Before Clodia could answer, Diana applied a damp rag to her face, sponging away dirt and dried blood. Clodia's breath caught at the gentleness of the touch. She closed her eyes, consciously steadying her breathing as the cloth passed over her bruised cheek and jaw.

After a few moments, Diana stopped, her hand falling into her lap. "You want to do this yourself?"

Clodia shook her head. She shrugged off the blanket she'd been wearing, to reveal her torn dress; she shivered as the cold air hit her skin. "If you could cut the bodice off," she said. "It'll be easier to mend later, than if we ripped it any further." Truthfully, she wanted to be rid of the horrid thing and all the memories it held, but she had no other clothing.

Diana rose and fetched a pair of scissors and a pile of grayish fabric. "I've an extra shirt you can wear for a shift," she said. "Just until the wh—ladies can find you a dress."

"My thanks." To distract herself from the warmth of Diana's big hands so close to her skin, she began to speak, and once she'd begun, she couldn't stop.

"I thought you were dead for sure," she said. "There was a bounty for you, dead or alive. I tried to get news, but nobody was allowed to see me. He had his man watching my door all the time, crazy jealous, you remember? Of course you remember. Aunt Livilla left me food while I was asleep, or sometimes one of the children would bring my rations. He wouldn't let me work my garden any more, not after one of the neighbors saw me and made some comment, I don't even know what."

She stopped abruptly, shocked out of her memories by Diana's hand, smoothing over her bare shoulder. Her bodice was gone, and her blanket had been laid in her lap. "What happened to make you run?" the younger woman asked. Diana's eyes were huge and dark.

Clodia had always thought if she tried hard enough, she could fall into those eyes and happily drown, except Clodia didn't deserve to take refuge there, after what she'd done. Diana didn't know yet, didn't realize how she'd come to this pass. Didn't know how she'd fallen. Clodia turned her face away from Diana's too-intimate gaze and said, "You left, that's what happened." She took up the blanket and wrapped it awkwardly around her.

Diana snorted. "Anybody who could run away did it. What did you expect me to do?"

"I wanted you to be free. But if he'd caught you, he'd of killed you. Killed you in front of me." Clodia covered her face with her hands. "You were gone and I had nothing any more. It felt worse than I expected it would. I thought I'd be happy you were free, and that would be enough. But I...I was selfish. I wanted you back, even when I knew it wasn't the right thing to want."

"Don't make it so complicated. Being a slave is as good as being dead," Diana said. "If I got killed when I ran, well at least I'd be free that way."

"You left me alone," Clodia whispered. "Before, I knew you were there. I couldn't see you, but I knew you were there. But then you were gone."

"I had to go," Diana said. Both her hands were on Clodia's

shoulders now. "I was dying inside."

"I know that. I don't blame you. I can't."

"I would've come back, when I could."

"And he would've killed you, like I said. I'm glad you left. But I hated you for leaving. And I loved you for leaving. Diana—"

"I can kill him for you." Diana's hand cupped her cheek, lifted her face. "I thought about it. I get sent scouting because I know this land. I can kill him for what he did to you, to all of us. I have a gun now, and they taught me how to use it. And he's the enemy. It would be easy. I wouldn't even have to get close."

"No," Clodia said, and though it hurt her aching muscles, she wrapped her arms around Diana and dragged her close, rough wool and gun oil and human warmth, the familiar scent that was all she'd ever had of home. "I was so angry at you."

Tentatively, Diana ran a hand over the shabby remains of Clodia's braids. "Are you still?"

Clodia couldn't answer. She let her head fall to Diana's shoulder and closed her eyes.

A long time later, Diana said, "Let's finish getting you cleaned up."

Clodia startled out of her half-doze. "I got out of the habit of being dirty," she admitted. "Being locked in that cabin all day, I didn't have much to do. I washed myself a lot, even though I could never wash quite enough to feel clean, you understand." She stopped suddenly and swallowed, not having meant to say so much. She didn't want to think of those days again. They were over. There was no use in dwelling, except to feel the pain all over again, and that was one thing she didn't need.

"I'll fetch you a bucket of water," Diana said. "Here's my cloth and soap. And—I thought of a way I can keep you safer. I can tell them we were married, and then I was sold off. It's a good story. They know I came from around here, but not from where exactly. And then I'll have a reason to keep you by me, for a while. They'll want to send you north as soon as they can, you being a woman, unless I can make a case for you staying on as a laundress or cook. But north wouldn't be so bad. There're people who helped me. They could help you, too. They weren't bad people. Quakers. You'd like them, they don't believe in fighting or killing."

Clodia flinched.

Diana stopped speaking, her gaze fastened on the ground. Diana had never been much of a talker, and Clodia was astonished she'd said so much all at one go. When Diana began to turn away, she touched her arm. "Thank you."

"I'll get you some clean water," Diana said again, awkwardly, before leaving.

Alone for a few moments, Clodia sagged, huddling into the army blanket. Her face throbbed, as did her side, and her heart. She'd never thought to see Diana again in this life, and when she did, she'd expected condemnation. She deserved condemnation for what she'd done...she had to tell Diana. She would find out soon enough, if the army lingered in this area. Clodia didn't dare think what might happen to her, and to Diana, if the army knew what she had done. They might not own slaves, but they were still white people in charge, and in her experience that always made a difference. Diana would forgive her, she knew, but would she help her? If it meant she might have to give up fighting in the army?

When Diana returned, carrying a bucket of clean water, Clodia had resolved to reveal all.

Diana set the bucket down and fastened the tent flap behind her. "I'll keep watch for you," she said, and turned her back. "Go on, it's only going to get colder."

Surprised, Clodia looked into the bucket. The water faintly steamed. "Thank you," she said, taking up the cloth and soap laid out for her. "Do you want me to save some for you?"

"Bathed this afternoon," Diana said. "While the officers was questioning you. They treat you all right?"

"They did. Even fed me." Clodia sighed deeply as the warm cloth met her skin. "This is heaven."

"Cheap at the price, then," Diana said. "The laundresses, they have plenty of hot water. I cut wood for them sometimes, carry heavy baskets. They were glad to do it. One of them's looking into some liniment, too, for those bruises."

The air chilled her wet skin. Shivering, Clodia shucked off the rest of her clothing, washing all over, then ducking into the shirt Diana had provided. "Done," she said, her teeth rattling. The sun had fallen below the horizon while they spoke. She could see the orange shadows of campfires through the tent's canvas walls. "Do you have to go?"

"No," Diana said. "I was on duty earlier. Now my job is to keep track of you. Which I'm doing." She took the bucket outside and dumped it. By the time she'd returned, Clodia was huddled beneath her blanket, trying to calm her shivering. "You all right?"

"Just cold," Clodia said. And tired. And sore. And almost sick with nerves. "I need to talk to you."

"You've been doing that all evening," Diana said, with a trace of humor. "I'd forgot how you could talk and talk and talk."

"I have something to tell you," Clodia said.

"Then it can wait until I'm under that blanket with you," Diana said. "It'll be warmer with the two of us, won't it?"

It would be. Warm and safe. While Diana shucked out of her uniform, Clodia asked, "Why were you so angry at me, when you first found me?"

"Wasn't."

"You were."

"Scared," Diana said, shortly. "You could tell them I was a woman. With this uniform, I have respect, and I can fight. I don't want to give that up."

"And?"

"Mostly that. And...I don't know." Diana, still wearing her long shirt, slipped under the blanket with Clodia, then threw her own blanket on top. Her arm pressed solidly against Clodia's, her head shared the same pillow. Then Diana turned on her side as well, facing Clodia, so they were closer still. "I thought, *you finally ran*, and I was furious you had waited so long. You wouldn't run when I asked you, when it would've been best, and yet here you were, beat all to hell. We could've been together all that time, but we weren't, and in the meantime...I didn't know what had happened to you. You might as well have been dead."

Clodia curled her arms close against her belly. "I was too scared to run when you asked me."

"I know. But I thought if *I* asked, if it was me—"

Clodia sighed. "We would've got caught together. I would've

held you back."

"Probably. It don't matter now." Diana reached out, tentative, and touched Clodia's arm. "Tell me what happened."

"After you left?"

"No, what made you run. Just get it out."

Clodia sucked in a deep breath. "I killed him."

Silence. Then, "How?"

"What? With, with my iron skillet."

"Good."

Diana was missing the important part. "If anyone finds out what I did. If the army finds out, your officers might...I don't know what they'd do. Would they hang me? For murdering a white man?"

"I'm sure not telling anybody. If you'd stayed, you'd be dead already. And he sure as hell deserved to get killed if anybody did." Diana tugged Clodia closer, insistently. Weak with relief, Clodia went, allowing Diana to tuck her head in close. She uncurled her arm and laid it around Diana's waist, and closed her eyes.

Clodia whispered, "After all the times I said it was wrong to kill. I still believe it's wrong. Taking a person's life, that takes away any chance they might have had for redemption. I sent that man straight to hell."

"He sent himself to hell. He was never going to change. He was beating on you, wasn't he? That's self-defense. You sure didn't get those marks on you from trees." Diana held her closer.

"I wasn't trying to kill him," Clodia said. "I just wanted him to leave me alone." She swallowed, then hesitantly admitted, "I was so scared. But I pretended I was you. And...I don't feel as awful about it as I think I should. I might not be as good a person as I thought I was."

"You did the only thing you could." Diana pressed her lips to Clodia's temple. "You've always been good, the best person I know. I'm proud of you."

"Even if I killed him by accident?"

"I don't care. He's dead, and you're safe. And I won't let anyone find out. If you're worried about what the Lord thinks, well, you can take it up with Him in private."

Clodia couldn't help it; she began to laugh, helplessly, her face buried against Diana's shirt. "I'll be sure and do that," she said, once she had enough air back to talk. She closed her eyes, limp with relief.

Diana's strong hand smoothed down her back. "You let me know if I'm hurting you, holding you so tight."

"Tighter," Clodia said.

"You sure?"

"Sure as I've ever been of anything." Clodia pressed her mouth to Diana's throat, not kissing exactly, just inhaling her. She took a deep breath and tasted her skin with the very tip of her tongue. Diana sucked in a breath. Clodia murmured, "Hold me. Show me you love me."

Diana clutched Clodia's hip and pulled her closer. "Do you know how many times I imagined I was your husband? That I was a man and I could have you for my wife?"

Clodia tilted her head back a little, trying to see Diana's face. "I never knew that."

"You knew I loved you."

"I did. You showed me, many a time. And I love you, Diana. Did I ever tell you that before?"

"Once. I held onto that, in the long nights. I hold onto it still."

Clodia smiled, burrowing against Diana's strong form. "You can hold onto *me* now."

For a long time, they were both silent. Clodia listened to the noises of the camp: she could hear occasional sounds from the animals picketed nearby, and sometimes a distant, low murmur of conversation. It was so dark she could no longer make out anything in the tent. Diana tugged their blankets higher, then muttered something about socks.

Clodia shifted her legs. Diana's cold feet pressed against her calves. "Better?" she whispered.

Diana's hand pressed into her back. The pressure felt wonderful on her sore muscles. "Did you mean it?"

"Mean what?"

"That I could hold onto you."

"You're doing that now," Clodia pointed out.

"Not what I meant. Would you...would you let me be like a husband to you? Hold you like that, and love you with my body?"

Clodia's eyes pricked with tears at the emotion in Diana's rough voice. "You have to ask me that? After everything?"

"Yes. Because I would never take that from you, if you didn't want to give it to me. You understand?"

"Oh, Diana. Oh, love."

There was nothing to do, then, but reach up and take Diana's face between her hands. Her cheeks were cold; they hadn't been beneath the blanket, or snugged up against a warm throat. Clodia couldn't see her face very well, but she bent close, so their noses just barely touched. "Yes. Yes and yes and yes." Diana didn't move, but her breathing sped up, warm gusts on Clodia's face. Clodia shifted, working herself partially free of Diana's embrace so she could straddle her body and bend low to brush their mouths together.

Their lips were chapped, and in the dark she wasn't as accurate at finding the other woman's mouth as she might have been in the light, but the contact was electric, sending a warm flush over Clodia's skin. Diana still hadn't moved, and she seemed to be holding her breath. Clodia kissed her again, pressing harder this time and slipping her tongue gently between Diana's lips until her mouth opened, and they were sharing breath.

Diana cupped Clodia's bruised cheek. Her hand was trembling. Clodia smiled, tears brimming in her eyes, and she let Diana pull her closer, their mouths meeting, melding.

A few minutes later, Diana wiped Clodia's cheeks with the back of her hand. "We're together now. We're free. It's all right, love."

"I know," Clodia said, sniffing. "I know. I'm just so happy. And you feel so good. And...after everything...I didn't think I could feel this happy."

Diana slid her arms around Clodia's back, stroking gently. "Come down here, if you can do that without hurting."

"Nothing hurts," Clodia said. "I'm so happy."

"I know. I know. So am I."

They held each other, their breath fogging the cold air of the tent. Diana said, softly, "Will you do something for me?"

"Anything."

"Would you call me *Dan*? I know *Daniel* is a man's name, and I wouldn't expect you to use that, but I needed to do it, you see. But I don't want to have to be reminded of my old life any more. Now I have you with me, I have all that was important from then."

"Dan," Clodia said. "I like that. It suits you."

"I never liked being called after some damned virgin." Dan rubbed her nose against Clodia's. "You sure it's all right? Us being like this? I was worried you would think it was wrong. That's why I never said anything."

Clodia thought about it. "More than all right," she said at last. "There is nothing bad about being here with you, like this. You make me feel safe." She laid her hand on Dan's face, so she felt the other woman's slow-growing smile. "I wish I could see your face right now."

"You'll get the opportunity tomorrow." Dan's hands slid down lower, her fingers curving into Clodia's waist. "Does that hurt?"

"I'm sore, but not too bad, not now," she said. "It feels good to have your hands on me, Dan. If it wasn't so cold, I'd want this shirt right off."

Dan squeezed her tighter and kissed her, more confidently this time. Clodia relaxed into it, and gradually began to feel warmer, even a bit flushed. What had been comfort started to become more than that. Dan's hands, big and strong as ever, were alternating pressing into her hips and circling on her rear, pressing them more closely together. It felt good, better even than when she pleasured herself. This was shared, this was them loving each other. The roughness of the shirts they wore, and the closeness of their embrace, made warm shudders cascade up and down her whole body. Her head and her belly were both dizzy with it. She shifted restlessly against Dan's strong body.

Dan. She liked that. A new name for a new life. Maybe she would choose a new name, too. But not now, when she couldn't think of much except getting closer to Dan.

Dan made a small sound in her throat, then whispered, "We've got to be quiet."

"Mmm." Clodia muffled her sound against Dan's shoulder. "I

need more of you. Will you touch me? Underneath this shirt. I want you to."

Dan made another small sound, this like a kitten's cry, and though it should have been funny to hear her make a noise like that, instead Clodia wanted to hear it again. Dan ran a hand down her arm. "You going to be warm enough if I do that?" Her voice shook.

"You'll just have to warm me up," Clodia said. "Will you let me touch you, too? The same way?"

"Lord, yes," Dan murmured. She sat up and yanked buttons of her shirt loose before shrugging it off her shoulders and arms. It pooled to her waist, and though there wasn't enough light to really see details, Clodia swallowed hard at the sight of all that bare skin, and Dan's small high breasts.

She sat up as well, running her hands down Dan's muscular arms. She'd always admired her friend's strength, inside and out. "Take this shirt off me," she pleaded.

Dan kissed her, hungrily, as if she couldn't stop herself, before she paused with her fingers on Clodia's buttons. She trailed her left hand down Clodia's chest, then squeezed her thigh before carefully unfastening her buttons, one, two, three, four. Cool air caressed her skin, swiftly followed by Dan's mouth and hands, licking and stroking.

It was awkward to struggle out of the shirts when they couldn't stop kissing each other, but they managed somehow, ending up facing each other beneath the blankets, Clodia braced on her uninjured side.

Dan touched Clodia's cheek again, looking into her face though she surely could not have seen her expression in the darkness. Dan traced down the line of her jaw and the side of her neck. Her hand came to rest on the upper slope of Clodia's breast, her thumb sliding back and forth until Clodia was driven nearly mad from it.

Dan said, "You're so soft. Softer than flower petals."

"More," Clodia murmured. "Put your mouth on me."

The kitten sound escaped Dan's throat again, and then she cupped both Clodia's breasts in her hands, bending close to nuzzle and nip and, finally, suckle. Clodia's fingers tangled in Dan's short curls. When Dan squirmed closer, hooking her leg over Clodia's hip, for a few moments they could do little but writhe against each other, beginning to sweat even in the cold.

Clodia gasped and whispered, "Let me touch you, too." She worked her hand down between them, following Dan's hipbone to her pussy, drifting her fingers through the nest of hair, tracing the slick seam, her breath catching in her throat as the tip of her first finger slid inside. She curled her finger, just a tiny bit, concentrating on the sweet texture, hot and slick, the tender inside of Dan. Clodia tried to speak, to tell her what she was feeling, but her throat closed and she had to choke off a sob of awe and joy. Slowly, she stroked her, then added another finger.

Dan made a noise, quickly burying it in Clodia's chest.

"I've got you," Clodia murmured, "Dan, love, do you feel me inside you?" She slid her fingers in more deeply, searching and caressing, finding the places that made Dan whimper and squirm, gradually moving her hand so she could work her thumb tenderly against Dan's clit while still fingering inside of her.

"Clodia, Clodia, Clodia," Dan was chanting, softly, the name soft puffs of air against Clodia's shoulder. Her muscles drew tight as a bowstring and she panted for air.

"I've got you," Clodia promised. "You want more, don't you? You need more to get to the other side?"

Dan's breath sobbed in her chest. Her hand dug into Clodia's side, hard enough to hurt, but Clodia didn't care. "Please. Please."

Clodia's eyes were wet. "Here, love. Grind on my hand, go on, take what you need. I've got you. I'm holding on to you like you held on to me."

Dan dragged in a sobbing breath and began to circle her hips. She was silent when she crested, but her leg clamped onto Clodia's, holding her tightly as she shook and gasped. Clodia felt like laughing as she tried to keep her hand from being crushed between them. *She* had done this. She had done this for Dan.

When Dan's muscles fell slack, she kissed Clodia, open-mouthed and sloppy. "Sorry," she whispered. "Wanted you to go first."

"Well, I wanted *you* to go first," Clodia replied. "I can't have you be doing every little thing for me." She extracted her hand from between them, shaking it to bring the feeling back.

Dan chuckled, sounding almost drunk. "Can I do one more little thing for you?"

"You can kiss my hand," Clodia said, breathlessly. "Me being a lady and all."

"You going to curtsey and tell me the weather's good for cotton?"

Clodia smiled and bumped their foreheads together. "If you're nice, I'm going to let you take advantage of me."

Dan took her hand, lacing their fingers together, then brought them both to her mouth. Clodia closed her eyes as Dan sensually slid her open mouth over their joined hands, then began to daintily clean with her tongue, as if she was a cat. "Oh, Lord," Clodia murmured.

Dan's tongue worked between her fingers, then she sucked one of those fingers between her lips, gradually suckling harder as she'd done with Clodia's nipples earlier in the evening. Clodia couldn't do anything but pant for breath, and restlessly squirm against Dan, trying to find more friction, more pressure just where she needed it.

Dan pulled her mouth away with a wet sound. "Yes. Just like that. You are so beautiful. You are the most beautiful woman I ever saw in my life."

"It's dark!" Clodia said, half-laughing, half-overcome with lust.

"I can see you with my hands," Dan said, using them to thumb Clodia's nipples, which were now so sensitive she could hardly bear the touch. "I want to make you come. You want me to make you come?"

"Fool," Clodia said, slapping at her clumsily. "Do it!"

"Just making sure," Dan said, mock-courteous. "Where do you want me to touch you?"

"Fool!"

Dan's hands traveled lower. "Guess you ain't up for no teasing right now."

Clodia bit her on the chin. Gently, but it was a demand.

Dan was laughing. "*There* you are," she said. "There you are, love. I found you. I'm going to find the inside of you now. Here's my hand. Feel my hand?"

Clodia grabbed the hand and crammed it against her pussy. "There," she said, firmly. "Rub me there."

"Yes, ma'am."

Clodia was beyond thinking clearly; she needed all her attention to breathe. Burying her face against Dan, she shifted her legs, opening herself to Dan's hand. The angle was awkward; Dan gently shifted Clodia onto her back and crouched above her. Cold air gusted under the blanket, a relief now on her hot skin instead of something to be endured. "Please, Dan," she said. "I want you inside of me. I want us joined."

Dan didn't tease any further, just slid fingers inside of her, working them in and out, her callouses a thrilling shiver. "You like that?" she asked.

"More," Clodia moaned.

Dan's other hand pressed against her mound. "That too much?"

"More."

Dan ground the heel of her hand against Clodia's clitoris, while the fingers of her other hand continued their inexorable thrusting. Clodia felt as if lightning sparked between the two points. Her legs twitched, out of her control; she panted and arched her back. More. She needed—more—"Ah!"

The pleasure ripped through her, chasing away thoughts, aches, fears, and all the while, Diana was with her. She never wanted it to end, but gradually her shudders slowed and eased, and she became aware of Dan's murmuring voice, close to her ear, and the gentle withdrawal of her hands from flesh now too sensitive to bear contact. "I love you, Dan," she said. "I love you so much."

Dan fell to the pallet beside her, snuggling up tight. "I found you," she said. "Oh, Clodia, I am so happy I found you."

Sleepily, happily, Clodia pressed a kiss to Dan's shoulder, the closest part of her she could reach. "So glad to be found. Dan. It's going to be all right."

Dan kissed her, soft and warm. "I'm going to make sure it is. From now on, I'll always find you."

"And I will find you," Clodia said.

There was still a war, and thousands were bound in slavery, and hatred lived everywhere. But Clodia had Dan, and Dan had Clodia. Together, they would never be lost again.

FORBIDDEN LOVE

BY J.B. HICKOCK

1900: The Boxer Rebellion: China

The Legation Quarter of Peking: two miles long and a single mile wide, bounded on one side by the Tartar Wall, the other near to the Imperial City.

Fires still burn in the city about the Legation, set by fanatical Chinese warriors. Even by this late date, flames mount from the Hanlin Academy, and drifting sparks rise from the national Library of China as books burn.

The day is July the 13th, the year 1900 in the common reckoning. The place is the Fu, a large palace and park where most of the few surviving Christian Chinese have taken refuge. Defended by the Japanese and Italian soldiers commanded by the indomitable Goro Shiba, on this day they have fallen back after bitter fighting against impossible odds, dropping back to their final defense line, exacting a bitter toll of the attackers, but never enough.

Bullets rip the air already rent by screams and shouts, the moans and whimpers of the wounded and dying. A family huddle in a hole as a party of soldiers race by. One of them, a Nipponese, sees them out of the corner of his eye and hurries back. He shouts at them to follow, reaching in and grabbing them when they don't move, too frightened to flee the coming fire.

Screaming in fear, two children are pulled out, one in each hand. The mother and father follow after them, trying to pry them free from him. In this way the soldier quickly draws out the whole family, booting and kicking them toward the Fu Palace—the last position they hold, and the only promise of safety.

His weather-beaten face screwed up in pain, he hurries after them, fighting not to limp even though the leg of his black trousers is stained red with blood. Chinese shouts and curses resound through the smoke-laden air. Glancing over his shoulder, the Japanese Marine tries to hurry. A heavy bullet spins out of the curling clouds of smoke to strike him. His teeth part as he cries out, spinning around from the force of the bullet and falling to the hard ground, clutching at his shoulder.

From out of the mist, a young nurse stumbles, following the sound of his cry. She is very tall and lithely built, wearing a simple light gray dress, a nurse's uniform, torn and dirty after weeks of siege. Her long red hair is bound in a tight braid now loosened, and long hairs fly about her dark eyes as she drops beside the wounded soldier, looking for the blood of his wound, almost invisible against the black of his uniform.

She hurriedly pulls away the thin chinstrap of his little cap, takes it off, and draws a pocket knife to cut away his uniform from the wound, moving with the assured ease of much experience gained since becoming a military nurse.

He mumbles something, and then fresh shouts and cheers split the air. The nurse whirls about to see a party of Chinese soldiers rushing toward them, doubtless moving toward the Fu but not about to pass by these two.

"No!" she cries, seeing the sharp points of spears and swords the Chinese point toward the wounded man, but they only laugh at her. Two of them grab her by the arms and drag her away. She turns her head, closing her eyes. She hears the Japanese soldier cry out, then the sickening sound of cutting flesh.

She stares about her in a panic as the Chinese soldiers surround their prisoner, pressing her back against a wall, almost alone in the smoke-shrouded field. These are some of the lesser Bannermen, like the raff and scaff of any army. Two of them grab her dress, ugly grins on their faces. "No!" she gasps. "Please, don't—"

A sharp order is snapped in Chinese. The soldiers hurriedly turn about and leap to attention. Looking past them, she sees a Chinese soldier of a very different sort.

Tall for a Chinaman, he is dressed in a long flowing robe, a sword and pistol belted at his waist, a tall hat upon his head. Clearly an officer, perhaps even a nobleman. Behind him, a long line of soldiers march toward the nearby gunfire; well-armed, disciplined men, very different from the Bannermen, as good soldiers as in any army.

The nobleman walks toward the small knot of Bannermen and their prisoner, followed by two soldiers, obviously bodyguards. He stares at the Bannermen for a long moment, then snaps another order.

Reluctantly, slowly, they turn and troop away, on toward the battle.

The nobleman turns to her and offers a slight bow. "I am sorry, Miss...?" he says in soft-spoken English.

"Guilford," she gasps, and remembers herself enough to curtsy in response to his bow. "Nancy Guilford."

"I am Yiquang, Prince Qing," he introduces himself.

Nancy's eyes widen in surprise. "Your Highness," she gasps, dropping into a deeper curtsy.

The Prince glances around. "You are a nurse?" he asks shortly.

"Yes," she says.

He nods, his eyes thoughtful, and says nothing for a long moment. "Come," he says, turning away. When she doesn't follow, he glances back at her. "I will take you to a safe place."

Nancy draws a deep breath, and follows. As she takes a step the earth shudders, and she nearly loses her feet. From not far away, Nancy hears a massive explosion. "What is that?"

"The French Legation is destroyed," the prince says calmly, not looking at her to notice the look on her face; she knew many people there. He takes her to a small party of his soldiers and speaks to them in Chinese too quickly for Nancy to follow. They glance toward the combat and, a little reluctantly, turn away from where their fellows are fighting to fall in around Nancy.

"Come," their sergeant says, in possibly his only English, and

Nancy comes. They walk away from the fighting, passing by the detritus of battle, dead and dying people, most of them Chinese, soldiers and Christians, shot down from the front or massacred. The sergeant orders his men away, and they return with a curtained palanquin. "Come," he says again, urging her into the chair.

Nancy sits within, and the curtains are drawn, cutting off her view of the city; then the conveyance trundles off, she knows not where. Along the way to her destination the cloth drifts aside, leaving a thin gap through which she can see. A masonry-faced wall towers over her, almost thirty feet high, and before them a gate looms, pierced by a row of nine by nine golden nails. Nancy cannot help but gasp in surprise and shock. She recognizes what she sees, though she has never been there before, she is being brought into the Forbidden Palace!

One of the soldiers glances over and sees the gap in the curtain. He reaches over and twitches it shut, closing her in blind darkness again. Although Nancy does not know it, she was brought through the West Glorious Gate into the Outer Court of the Forbidden City. With Prince Yiquang's orders, his soldiers can easily pass even there without question.

In short order, they bring her into the Inner Court, where the Imperial family lives and the business of government is carried on. The palanquin stops and the curtain is flipped back. "Come," the sergeant says. The soldiers lead her into a large palace building, down a long hall and into a room.

Nancy is taken aback by the sight of the room: brilliantly lit, with expensive hangings and rugs, the room is dominated by a large soft bed in which a woman lies. Prince Yiquang stands by the bed, looking down at her. He glances up at Nancy's entrance, orders the soldier out, and turns to her as the door closes. "Welcome to the Forbidden City." He glances at the woman in the bed, who seems in the fit of an uneasy sleep. "This is Chen Yun Huan, an Imperial Concubine. I need her cared for, and here you will be safe." Before Nancy can say a word, he turns and strides out. The door shuts behind him, and she hears bolts being thrown.

Nancy turns away from the door and walks over to the bed.

Huan has a pale heart-shaped face with long dark lashes and soft red lips beneath a small upturned nose. Her forehead is creased, as if with pain. Her eyes open wide, long lashes fluttering, and she looks up at Nancy out of wide brown eyes. At the sight of the strange woman she flinches away. "Shh, shh, it's all right," Nancy says in her best Chinese, gently laying her hands on Huan's shoulders. "I'm here to help you."

Huan's eyes flash about the room and, realizing that she has not been moved, she relaxes, but still stares at Nancy suspiciously.

"Prince Yiquang bought me here to help you," Nancy says, sitting on the bed beside her. Huan relaxes a little more at the mention of the prince's name. "Tell me, please, what hurts?"

The concubine pulls her right hand out from under the covers and presses it to her breast. "Here," she says softly, her voice low and sweet.

Nancy nods, then grabs the covers and slides them aside. "I have to see," she says to Huan. Beneath the covers, Huan wears a light robe. She does not protest as Nancy unbinds it and opens the robe to bare her breasts. Nancy notes idly that they are small, very different from an occidental's, as she reaches down with her hands upon Huan's chest above her breasts. The Chinese woman hisses when Nancy's cold fingers brush her soft skin. "Oh, sorry," Nancy says, then rubs her hands together to warm them. She places her hands on Huan's chest and rubs her soft flesh gently. "Does this hurt?" she asks,

Huan shakes her head. "No."

Nancy frowns, rubbing her hands lower, her fingers brushing the sensitive flesh of Huan's breasts. "Does this hurt?"

"No," Huan moans softly.

Nancy glances down and sees Huan's breasts, her nipples grown hard and erect under the unintended caresses. The two women glance at each other, neither knowing what to say. Each is intimately aware of how their warm bodies press against each other.

Nancy clears her throat and takes her hands away. "Are you hot?" she asks, placing the back of her hand against Huan's forehead, finding it hot with fever.

"No," the sick woman says with a shiver. "I am cold."

"Does it hurt to breathe?" Nancy asks with a frown.

Huan shakes her head. "No," she says. "I just feel cold."

Nancy presses her ear to Huan's chest, aware of how she lies against the concubine's breast. "Breathe, please," she says. Her own warm breath brushes over Huan's sensitive flesh, making her moan as the warm air flows past her hard nipple.

Obediently, Huan takes a deep breath, then lets it out.

Nancy straightens up, frowning again. The poor woman has a bad case of influenza, but why had she not been treated before now? Why did the Prince bring a westerner here to treat her? It makes no sense. Clearly, there are things happening in the Forbidden Palace that are beyond her. Nancy throws that question aside, knowing she will never find out.

Quickly, she closes Huan's robe, tying it tightly, her fingers once more brushing across her breasts. She pulls the covers back over her, then turns, rising off of the bed to walk to the door and knock on it. After a moment the bolts are thrown back and the door opens a crack to let a soldier peer in. "I need medicines," Nancy says, and lists them.

The soldier stares back at her for a long silent moment, then shuts the door again.

A distant explosion penetrates to this room. Nancy glances toward the curtained windows, wondering where the gunfire is landing, before turning back to Huan on the bed. The young lady, no older than Nancy, looks up at the westerner as she comes back to the bed. "I am sick," Huan says, staring at her. "Will I die?"

"Maybe." Nancy sits down beside her patient.

The concubine is silent for a long while, her eyes lowered in thought. She glances back up at Nancy. "If you are found here, you will die."

"Yes."

"I hope you are not found."

"Thanks," Nancy says with a grin. "I hope you don't die, too."

The bolts of the door are thrown back with a clatter. They look and see it open just enough to permit a small tray to be slid in, then slammed shut again.

The tray proves to hold the medicines that Nancy requested.

She carries it back to the bed and hurriedly measures out a spoonful. Huan opens her mouth and Nancy slides the spoon in, but a drop of the amber liquid drops on her chin. "Sorry," Nancy says, and reaches down with her left hand to wipe it away. She freezes, her fingers resting on Huan's chin.

Huan stares into her eyes. She reaches up and takes Nancy's hand in her own, gently caressing her long thin fingers. "You are very pretty," she says.

Nancy ducks her head, a flush rising in her cheeks. "Thank you," she says, I—" She stops and turns away, reclaiming her hand from Huan's grip, returning the medicine and spoon to the tray. She takes up a jar of oil and returns. With the covers thrown back once more, she opens up Huan's gown before spreading the oil on her hands and looking down at the Chinawoman's soft young breasts.

A little reluctantly, disturbed, confused, feeling something strange, Nancy reaches down and gently lays her hands on Huan's chest. Huan draws in a deep breath, her breasts rising as the cool oil touches her warm skin. Confusion is in her own eyes, and a glint of something...welcoming, Huan looks up and meet's Nancy's gaze. Nancy slowly runs her hands over Huan's chest, rubbing the oil into her smooth skin.

Huan's eyes close and she moans softly with pleasure as Nancy's hands move over her, long fingers pressing down on her soft flesh, rubbing the oil in, squeezing her breasts. Nancy rubs her fingers over every inch of her chest. Huan's lips part in a gasp when Nancy's fingers flick her nipples. "Oh!" she moans. Nancy presses her hands close against Huan's breasts, gently squeezing. Huan moans as Nancy kneads her soft flesh, gently pinching her nipples between her fingertips. Suddenly Huan reaches up and grabs Nancy, pulling her down into a kiss.

It is a quick light kiss, soon over. Nancy pulls herself away, staring down at Huan in surprise. Huan looks back up at her nervously, waiting for her response. In truth, Nancy herself does not know how to respond. Her lips part as if to speak, but she can think of nothing to say.

"Well?" Huan asks nervously.

Nancy gently places her hands on Huan's shoulders, then

leans down until their lips meet, and part, and their tongues slide gently, hesitantly, over each other, tasting each other for the first time.

They break apart and gaze into each other's eyes. Nancy is unsure, surprised, even confused, but Huan smiles up at her. "In the palace, friendships are common."

Nancy gapes at her. By *friendship* she can't mean...could she? But whatever is meant, Huan is still weak and sick. Nancy gives her a smile, then carefully rearranges her covers.

The next day Nancy measures out another portion of medicine and spoons it into Huan's mouth. She stares with concern at her patient, worry in her eyes. Huan's color has worsened; her cheeks and brow burn a bright red, and her fever seems higher. She stares up at Nancy with befogged eyes, as if lost in a dream, and murmurs quietly to herself, moaning about her parents, lost, taken from her, and a boy's name—perhaps memories of a life before she was taken.

A meal is brought by the soldiers and placed on the floor by the door. Nancy turns away from the bed to pick up the tray and brings it back with her. It seems to be some kind of noodles and vegetable soup; beyond that she doesn't care. Sitting on the bed beside Huan, Nancy scoops up some of the soup and spoon feeds it to her patient.

Huan swallows the soup that Nancy slips into her mouth, but turns away with a sick moan when Nancy tries to give her the noodles. Nancy takes the noodles away, and gives her the last of the soup before taking the noodles and eating some of them herself. After all, she cannot nurse her patient if she has no strength.

After eating, Huan lies still, seemingly asleep, but her breath comes shallow and sharp, as if she has just run a great distance. Nancy looks down at her patient, deep concern and worry shining in her eyes. She knows that a fever like this can only burn itself out, but it could easily burn out the sufferer first, if she doesn't have the strength to resist, and Huan looks weak as she lies there with the quilted covers pulled up to her chin.

Nancy takes a small cloth and folds it into a pad, then fills a bowl with water. She sits back on the bed beside Huan, the pad in her hands and the bowl set within easy reach, and dips the pad in the water, then dabs gently at Huan's sweaty brow, rubbing the sweat away, cooling her fever. Huan murmurs something that sounds grateful as Nancy wets the cloth and resumes dabbing her brow again. "It's okay," Nancy says softly in her best Chinese. Not in a proper dialect, but learned haphazardly from her patients in the church mission. "You'll be fine," she says softly, a promise she doesn't know if she can keep. But as she looks down at Huan's pained features, she feels determined that it shall be made true.

She continues to dab at Huan's brow, but it is only a temporary palliative, not a real treatment. She lays the bowl and cloth aside, turns back to the meal tray, and sits on the edge of the bed, sternly slipping noodles into her mouth, staring intently at Huan's face. She seems to have fallen into a shallow sleep, breathing unevenly, her breasts rising and falling, her closed eyes twitching as if she struggles through some fevered dream. Setting aside the remains of the meal, Nancy turns to Huan again. Feeling her brow makes Nancy frown in worry. Her body still is heating itself, struggling to warm itself even further. Sweat stands out thickly on her face, evidence of the effort her body is going through, and if she cannot slow down her body's efforts, she may literally burn herself from the inside.

Nancy takes up a shallow cup of water, then braces Huan's shoulder with her left arm, holding the cup in her right hand, and lifts Huan up. Huan moans, shivering as the covers fall away slightly.

"Shh, shh, you're doing fine," Nancy says, raising the cup to her parched lips. Huan swallows the water greedily, sucking at the lip of the cup until it is all gone. Nancy refills the cup, and sets it back to Huan's lips until she has swallowed it all again.

Putting the cup aside, Nancy settles Huan back down on the pillow. In seconds she falls back into her uneasy sleep. Nancy then pulls back a corner of the covers and, still fully clothed, crawls beneath them to lie beside Huan. Huan moans in her sleep as Nancy's body comes to rest beside her own. The nurse settles the covers over them both, then presses herself against Huan, trying to pour her own body's warmth into the sick woman's, to help her grow warm without extra effort. In minutes, Nancy is sweating almost as much as Huan herself, but she can feel Huan growing a little less tense, her shivers growing a little less strong. She rests her head against Huan's shoulder, and closes her eyes.

Nancy awakens a long time later and sits up, glancing around. The room is dark and still, night having fallen in the interim. Soft lantern light shines amid the darkness outside, its glow filtering into the room through the curtained windows. She turns and glances at Huan, the soft features of her face outlined in the dim light. Hitching herself up on one elbow, Nancy feels her forehead and the back of her neck. Huan's brow is cool, her eyes closed and still. Her fever has broken, and she lies at ease, breathing deeply, peacefully asleep.

Nancy heaves a sigh of relief and curls herself close to Huan. Wrapping her arms around the concubine, the nurse pulls her close and falls asleep again with her cheek pressed to the other's shoulder.

Nancy is awoken by Huan stirring beside her. The concubine is sitting up, holding the covers to her breasts, looking around as if in surprise, perhaps waking from a dream. Her wandering eyes meet Nancy's, and memories come flooding back. She rolls over, bringing herself closer to Nancy. "Thank you," she says, leaning close until their lips meet. Heat rises in Nancy's body, responding to Huan's kiss and caresses, as Huan grasps at Nancy's clothing, reaching for her bare flesh.

They part for air, and Huan pulls open Nancy's dress. "How do you find yourself?" she giggles, easing her fingers down beneath Nancy's petticoats to rest on her mound, their tips stroking her gently. Nancy moans, her eyes closed as Huan strokes her, slipping a finger inside, then two, gently rubbing the soft place between her legs.

Huan rolls Nancy over onto her back, and slides on top of her. Nancy looks up at Huan's naked body, her breasts hanging just above her head. Huan looks down at her with a wide smile, then leans down and kisses her, first on her mouth, then the chin, then in the hollow of her neck, and down between her breasts.

Nancy moans softly as Huan's lips ghost across her naked belly, and lower, between her legs. Huan easily slips her petticoats away, baring her to the air, making her shiver as the warm air blows across her sensitive flesh, until Huan's lips slide between her thighs. Nancy stiffens, then shivers as Huan slides her warm wet tongue between her lower lips, darting its tip back and forth, exploring Nancy's creases, gently caressing her clit. Nancy moans, throwing her head back, her curly red hair, loosed from its binding, spreading about her head like a halo.

Huan slips her tongue deep into Nancy, in and out, sliding the wet tip against the hard nub of her clit, dampness increasing in response. Then she draws back, licking her lips, staring down at Nancy with a smile. "Don't stop!" Nancy gasps, and Huan plunges back into her.

Nancy moans with pleasure and relief. Days, weeks of uncertainty and fear, all slip away as a flaming tide rises beneath Huan's tongue. Even the memory of the siege drops away as her whole being narrows to this single moment, the single point of sensation that fills her until she feels about to explode...shudders...and cries out in pleasure.

Huan draws back again and watches as Nancy slowly comes down from the heights of ecstasy, her eyes half-lidded with pleasure.

Still smiling, Huan crawls up Nancy's body once more until she straddles her chest, kneeling on the bed, her damp naked crotch before Nancy's lips.

Nancy glances up at Huan for a short moment, then opens her mouth wide. Huan eases forward the few inches, pressing her soft shaven flesh against Nancy's wide-open mouth. Nancy tastes Huan's arousal as a drop of her juices brushes against her waiting tongue. "Mmmm." Nancy moans. She had never done that, not to another woman. But Huan loves it, shivering and moaning herself, grinding against Nancy's face, inviting her to taste more.

Nancy slides her tongue along Huan's opening, her lips sucking gently, her vision filled by Huan's hot sweaty skin. Huan shivers and wriggles against her. Nancy licks her again, easing her tongue past the folds of her soft skin and inside her. Ignorant, not knowing what she is doing, she lets Huan guide her, feeling her quiver and sigh with pleasure as Nancy finds the perfect spot.

Huan gives a soft cry as Nancy sucks and licks at her, exploring the limits of her tight wet opening, losing herself in the moment as she drives Huan higher and higher on a tide of excitement until she shudders once more and gives a muffled scream as she comes to a climax of pleasure.

Neither woman says anything about it afterward, but they lie together beneath the covers, naked, their bodies pressed closely together. They stare closely into each other's eyes, neither knowing what to say. They have so many differences, so many things to keep them apart. A distant murmur of gunfire sounds, as if to drive the point home.

Nancy closes her eyes and presses herself against her beloved Huan. Whatever happens, let it just happen tomorrow, she thinks to herself.

Huan and Nancy are awoken by shouts from outside the door. The two women clutch at each other, staring in fright at the door as the bolts are thrown back.

Remembering herself, Nancy gets to her feet, taking a long step away from Huan, clutching her dress about herself as the door swings open and a nobleman steps in. He stands in the doorway and sweeps the room with a stern gaze. He wears impressive robes of state, a long sword belted at his waist, his hand resting aggressively on the hilt.

Huan gasps. "Prince Duan," she cries, her eyes wide with horror.

Nancy's eyes flicker from the prince to Huan and back again. Prince Duan, one of the most powerful men in China, leader of the Tiger and Divine Corps. Behind him stand several of his soldiers, tall strong men armed with modern rifles. They stare at her with open hostility in their dark eyes. Selected from the finest of the Bannermen, they burn with loyalty to the Emperor and hatred of the foreigner.

Prince Duan points at Nancy. "Take her," he orders in Chinese.

"No," Huan cries out as two of his men rush forward and grab the nurse. "No, please!" Huan screams as they bear her away. The concubine clambers weakly to her feet, clutching her robe about herself. "No, she saved my life," she cries as the Prince turns away. "Don't do this!"

The door is slammed in her face.

The Dowager Empress Cixi's throne room. A large round room, well-lit but built from a dark stone that lends the room a dark, dangerous air. A small pillow rests on the floor before the Imperial Throne for supplicants to kneel upon. George MacDonald had contemptuously kicked it aside and given a Western bow, determined that the representative of the British Empress would stand before the Chinese Empress.

When she is brought there, Nancy drops to her knees before the throne, tears of fear shining in her eyes.

Empress Cixi leans forward in her throne and stares down at the cringing Occidental, her heavy robes of state hanging on her frame like the wings of an aged bird, old but still full of spirit. Her dark eyes flash over Nancy, glittering with intelligence, but not alight with mercy. "The only penalty for entering the Forbidden Palace is death," Prince Duan is saying. He looks happy, and well he might. Finding the westerner in the Forbidden Palace has brought him honor at the expense of his rival, Yiquang.

Nancy sobs. She lowers her head to the floor, pressing her

forehead to the cold stone. "Please have mercy!" she sobs in her broken Chinese. In a far corner of her mind, she realizes how pathetic she must look. But she has seen so much of killing and dying in Peking. And she really, really wants to live.

The Empress's lips press together in a thin line, perhaps offended that the conversation between Empress and Prince is interrupted. "It is as you say, Prince Duan," she says.

Nancy moans in fear.

"Let her be boiled alive," the Empress orders.

Nancy raises her head, eyes wide with horror. Prince Duan turns to her with a smile and gestures to his men. Nancy gasps as they grab her. "No, please!" Once more, she is taken away.

In a dark prison cell, Nancy lies on her back, staring blankly at the ceiling above. A small lantern hangs in a corner, throwing a few lighter shadows across the dark room. Other than that it is a bare stone room, no window, no sign of the passage of time: it could have been days since she was thrown in here.

Without any warning the bolt of the door is thrown back, and it opens. Her heart pounding in her ears, Nancy sits up, staring fearfully at the dark figure outlined in light. Then her eyes adjust to the brightness and her eyes widen in recognition. "Huan," she cries.

The concubine drops to her knees beside the prisoner and wraps her arms around her. "I'm sorry," she sobs, pulling Nancy close. "I couldn't do anything!"

Nancy hugs her close.

They break apart for a moment to look into each other's eyes.

"How did you get in here?" Nancy gasps. "I thought..."

"I bribed a guard," Huan says with lowered eyes.

A shiver runs through Nancy's body. She closes her eyes, squeezing them shut to hold back tears. "I don't want to die!"

Huan leans close to press her lips to Nancy's. This is no chaste peck, but a lover's kiss. Nancy responds, and their tongues twine and dance around each other, tasting and testing each other, perhaps for the last time.

Huan finally breaks it off with a gasp for breath. "Come here," she says hoarsely, easing Nancy down in her arms, laying the captive on her back on the floor. Nancy looks up at Huan in the dim light, her eyes shining as Huan stands, hands dropping to the fastenings of her dress.

She lets it slide down off of her body, shivering as the soft silk glides over her warm skin. She wears nothing beneath, and stands in the cool air. "I will give you something to remember," she promises, her voice ragged and trembling with emotion. "Something to keep you warm here, and in the next life." The dim lantern light shines on her skin as she lowers herself over Nancy to sit with her knees to either side of Nancy's head. "Now," she says softly. "Pleasure me."

Nancy opens her mouth wide and raises her head to press her lips to Huan's flesh. She slides her tongue out, slipping it through Huan's folds. She moans softly as her tongue easily finds the hard little nub of Huan's clit, and feels Huan shiver as she flicks at it.

Her breath coming hard as Nancy licks her, Huan leans down, pressing the length of her naked body to Nancy's, supporting her own weight with her hands, brushing her hanging breasts against Nancy's belly. She gathers up Nancy's skirt and pulls it away to bare her legs, her lower belly, the soft place between her thighs, already damp with arousal and expectation. Her lips part in a gasp of pleasure, and then she lowers herself to press her lips to Nancy.

Nancy shudders as the soft wet tip of Huan's tongue slides between her damp folds. She consciously thrusts aside any thought of the short future, and redoubles her efforts with her tongue, throwing her whole being into this precious moment. Huan arches her back. Nancy drives her tongue against her clit. "Oh! Good—!" Huan never finishes the thought, her cry ending in a keening whimper.

Nancy shudders, her full breasts moving as she struggles beneath Huan's naked weight. "Mhmm," she moans as Huan drives her own tongue back down into her, sucking with her lips, pressing them to her flesh in a kiss of passion.

"Ahhh," Huan cries out, her small breasts swaying as she

throws her head back. Nancy thrusts her tongue ever harder into her, sucking at Huan's juices, driving pleasure into her lover, making her squirm and moan.

"Mmm!" Nancy's muffled voice rises shrill and loud, her whole body shaking, sweat sheening her naked skin as Huan grinds her tongue deep, forcing her to a stormy climax.

Nancy's tongue returns the favor, making Huan squirm, her voice rising louder and higher, losing words, until with an inarticulate cry of pleasure as she comes. Huan collapses atop of Nancy, then turns to wrap her arms around her, rubbing their naked skin together, looking deeply into her eyes.

Sikh soldiers march proudly into the Legation quarter, cheered by the defenders; the Indian soldiers and their British officers had marched and fought across half of China with the combined army to relieve the siege. Amidst the cheering crowds of Westerners and Chinese Christians, Nancy watches them pass, feeling ambivalent: she is surely happy to be alive, but what will become of China after this? On the same day that she sentenced Nancy to death, the Dowager Empress received word of the victory of the Eight-Nation Alliance in the field. The powerful modern army was descending on Peking even as Nancy was cast into her dark cell. Not desiring to antagonize the victors, Empress Cixi ordered Nancy to be held, but not executed, and ended the direct attacks on the Legation Quarter .

The Dowager Empress had fled at the approach of the Alliance, leaving Prince Ronglu, a moderate, to hold the Capitol and negotiate with the victorious foreigners for a peace treaty. The Prince had released Nancy, letting her back into the Legation Quarter for protection. Most of the Boxers have scattered, disillusioned, and returned to their homes. Nationalism will rise again, for the Chinese are a proud people, but it will be reborn based on rationalism, and hopefully will grow with respect for all people, regardless of religion. Nancy heard that twenty thousand Christians were massacred in Peking, men, women, and children. Only a few thousand survived by taking refuge with the Westerners in the Legation Quarter and the Northern Cathedral, where they had suffered through their own fierce siege.

Nancy gasps as a hand is laid on her shoulder. "What—" she cries out as she is pulled back, away from the crowd, into a small alley. She opens her mouth to scream, then her lips are covered, and she stares into familiar brown eyes inches from her own. Nancy surrenders to the soft grip that holds her, melting against Huan's body, her lips parting to return the kiss laid on them.

They break apart to stare closely into each other's eyes, still wrapped in each other's arms. "I never thought I'd see you again!" Nancy gasps.

Huan smiles. She has put off the burnished silks of the Imperial Palace in favor of simple cotton, free from the gilded cage. "Well, I'm here," she says, then draws Nancy close again.

However uncertain the future, they'll face it together.

DELIVERY

BY VICTORIA JANSSEN

1916: WWI: France

The driver was tall and lanky, and at first Matilda thought she was a man; her blonde hair was cropped short and mostly concealed beneath a cloth cap. The cap highlighted high cheekbones and plush lips. She wore trousers and a baggy knitted jumper, with a pistol belted low. It was only the curve of hips beneath the embossed holster that truly revealed her sex. "Miss Graves?" she said brusquely. "I've come to fetch you."

Matilda stood up slowly and unkinked her back. She'd been sitting on the trunk full of telephone equipment for several hours, and her long wool overcoat had been insufficient against the bitter autumn wind. Adding to her inner chill, the ground shook periodically from distant shelling, unnerving her.

When she'd left England to escort the trunk to Le Havre, no one had told her she'd be escorting it all the way to Colonel Ellis, encamped in a ruined village near one of the Base Hospitals. She'd been ready for an adventure, but only a minor one. If she'd known she was in for a real adventure, she would have worn sturdier shoes, and perhaps some additional long underwear, she thought wryly.

She'd been told soldiers would be detailed to transport the much-needed equipment, with His Majesty's thanks to her and her small engineering company. No one had deigned to tell her what had prompted the change in plan; she'd been lost in a sea of soldiers disembarking, and other soldiers, these on stretchers, being loaded onto the ship. She'd suspected the driver of the first lorry, the one that had found her at the port and then dropped her here, had not known any details. He'd only said, affably, that he had orders, and someone else would come for her presently. That had been some hours ago, and twilight was now rapidly descending on the French countryside. It was clear she would not be heading home until tomorrow, at least. She tried not to think of all the things that could go wrong between now and the morning.

"I'm Miss Graves," Matilda said. She wondered how she would explain herself, if asked. Spinster engineers did not normally travel into war zones, and this woman did not seem as if she would be tolerant of hesitation.

The driver seemed satisfied with just her name. "Cynthia Carpintero," she said. "Let's get your trunk loaded." Her voice had a pleasant low rasp, like a cup of strong tea. Belatedly, Matilda realized the driver's flat accent was American and, a moment later, that her vehicle was an ambulance, its paneled side painted with a large red cross. Probably it belonged to the base hospital near Colonel Ellis's headquarters. Some of the telephone equipment was destined for the hospital. That was one of the reasons Matilda had been glad to contribute her effort.

It felt good to be moving. Her hands, stiff with cold even through her leather gloves, slipped on the trunk's smooth straps before she found her grip. Impressively, Carpintero lifted her end with no apparent effort and dragged the trunk and Matilda both toward the rear of the ambulance, which smelled overwhelmingly of carbolic. The trunk fit snugly between the two rows of patient berths lining the ambulance's interior, with some shoving; Carpintero took care to fling a couple of blankets over it before shutting the rear doors. "Let's go," she said.

Matilda had rather been hoping the cab of the ambulance might be warm. Once inside, she settled for being out of the wind; cold air leaked up through the floorboards and chilled her feet through the thin soles of her boots. Carpintero handed over a scratchy wool blanket, also smelling of carbolic, and a thermos. "Coffee. Might still be hot."

"Thank you." She sipped cautiously while Carpintero released the brake and worked the throttle, flipping a lever for the spark. The coffee was harsh, bitter, and blessedly scalding. She draped the blanket over her lap, wishing her constricting skirt would allow her to tuck her frozen feet up. It wasn't a fashionable hobble skirt, but it was also far from the flowing skirts of her youth, mostly because fabric had grown so dear, and the girls grew out of clothing in mere months, it seemed.

The ambulance lurched forward. Carpintero cursed fluently enough to make Matilda blush as they bumped across cavernous ruts. It was true she thought such words, but she never let them escape her mouth. She supposed if she cursed here, no one at home would know. It was a strange but freeing thought.

Finally, they were progressing along what might optimistically be termed a road and Matilda dared to take another sip of the horrid, ambrosial coffee. "How far is it?" she asked.

Carpintero replied without shifting her gaze. "Maybe six hours? This isn't one of my regular runs, this is extra. I'm usually running patients from the aid stations to the Base Hospital."

Farther than Matilda had hoped for, but not the distance she'd feared. She resigned herself to getting no sleep this night. "Are you acquainted with Colonel Ellis?" she asked.

Carpintero laughed. "Not had the, umm, pleasure. He don't associate with the lady doctors at the hospital, and even less with us drivers. He's made it plain he don't—doesn't—think women belong over here at all." She paused. "I was right surprised to learn I was supposed to bring you to him."

"I wasn't meant to be here," Matilda explained. "There was to be an officer—"

"Oh," Carpintero said. "I bet it was that young adjutant of his. Got himself killed last night, some sniper while they was out fixing wire." She imparted the dire information as if speaking of the weather.

"I didn't realize the encampment was so close to the Front,"

Matilda said, striving to ignore a sudden weakness in her knees. She drew a deep, slow breath. It wasn't that she was a coward, exactly. She just needed time to get used to the idea of men killing each other within a few miles of her present position.

"Isn't that close. Don't worry, I won't let you get blown up."

"Thank you?"

Carpintero laughed. "We'd have to be mighty lucky to get pulverized this far back. I mean, those Germans have to be real lucky to hit us."

"I am infinitely reassured." Matilda tucked the thermos between them on the bench seat and tucked her cold hands beneath her arms. She realized she was enjoying speaking to the other woman; she was easy to talk to, and reminded her of how long it had been since she'd last had a woman friend, other than her sister-in-law. She said, "I was hoping to return safely home with exaggerated tales of danger and glory for my young nieces. They are no doubt in a state of high excitement right now, if they've learned I won't be back tomorrow morning, as expected. I shan't have to exaggerate as much as I thought."

"They live with you?" Carpintero asked.

"Yes, with their mother. My brother was killed at Neuve Chapelle." How easily the words came now, as if they meant nothing. And in the face of so many deaths since then, her own loss was nothing special. She had given up any thought of the grief ever easing.

"I'm sorry."

The phrase was brief, but Matilda felt the sincerity of it. "Thank you. It isn't so bad for us. I have a salary from my company, and my sister-in-law a pension. The girls—there are three—are in school."

"My brothers all have boys," Carpintero commented. "Nine in all."

"Nine!"

"Noisy as all get out, especially when we're all together for Christmas and the like. I'm from Arizona," she added. "We got made a real state in '12."

"That's...in the west? There are cowboys there?"

Carpintero laughed long and loud, like light in the darkness. "You might say that, but I wouldn't. Cowboys got a bad name due to some of them cowboy desperados back when my daddy was young. My family are ranchers, except a few of my brothers, they've gone to work for the railroads, and my next youngest brother, Daniel, he's gone in on a copper mine."

"And you?" Matilda asked. "What sort of work do you do, in Arizona?" She'd wondered about America, sometimes. Women couldn't vote there, or not yet, but she'd heard a great deal about business opportunities on the frontier. Rapid urbanization would provide a prime market for companies such as hers, which created and assembled specialized telephone and telegraph equipment. Were the women there all like Miss Carpintero? That would be something to see.

"Me? Well, Miss Graves, I worked as a cowboy—not the desperado kind—for my daddy, even though he and Ma would rather I got married and had some kids. I don't think I want none, though. I think my brothers have done taken care of that already. You married?"

"No. I never had the time."

"Or wanted it?" Carpintero's voice was suddenly much quieter.

Matilda took a deep breath. Usually she managed to avoid discussing it, but here, it seemed safe to do so. "No. No, I never really wanted to marry. I wouldn't mind children of my own, I suppose. Someday. But I just can't imagine..."

"Me, neither. I always felt more like I should've been a man. I like being free and deciding things for myself."

For a few moments, there were no sounds beyond the rattle of the ambulance on the road, and the distant shelling. "That's it, exactly," Matilda said. "I...I have always wondered how my life would have been different, had I been born male. If I had been the one groomed as a solicitor..." She stopped. "Though I suppose had I been born male, I likely would be dead now, like Kenneth."

"I'm sorry," Carpintero said, again. "I don't mind admitting I'm glad America doesn't have a dog in this fight, since all but two of my brothers are just the right age to get taken for the army."

Matilda didn't want to dwell on brothers or the losing of them. "But you became an ambulance driver. You traveled all the way from Arizona to France."

"I did. Thought I could do some good over here. Learned all about automobiles working on the ranch—we use them sometimes instead of horses—and I saved up money and bought my own. This one." She patted the steering wheel. "The ladies at the Base Hospital were real happy to have me, even though I'm not educated like them. I can fix all the ambulances, you see, not just my own. They like having more women around the place, too. They feel like it avoids what they call disrupting influences." She paused. "I know that sounds like they're a bunch of prim old ladies, but they're not. Those lady doctors can stitch up and amputate better than any man."

"Except for the amputations, it sounds lovely," Matilda said, envious.

Carpintero chuckled.

Matilda imagined what it would be like to go into the office each day and find only women waiting for her. She would not have to check her clothing and straighten her spine each day as she stepped through the front doors of her own company, to ensure she remained impeccable under the gazes of five men of her father's generation.

Perhaps, next time an additional clerk was needed, she might see if a woman was available for the position. There was no lack of women working in Birmingham at the moment.

She hadn't expected to be having these thoughts here, in France, in the dark, in an ambulance with an American cowboy. "Tell me more about Arizona," she said. "What does it look like? Does everyone go about armed?"

Two hours later, the darkness had become impenetrable except directly before the headlamps of the ambulance, and Matilda and the driver had progressed to addressing each other by their Christian names. For long stretches, Matilda had forgotten she was in France. She had forgotten everything except Cynthia sitting next to her, lean and blonde and tanned, her raspy voice caressing Matilda's skin in the dark.

Not so long ago, Matilda had boarded at school for the years of her father's last illness. Homesick, lonely, worried for her family, she'd spent many long nights speaking quietly to the other girls in the dark, sometimes over smuggled biscuits, sometimes huddling beneath the same blankets. She'd had a particular friend, for a few months, an older girl named Hanna, sent to school while her guardianship and inheritance were hashed out in the courts.

Hanna had loved dresses and especially hats, but unlike the other girls, she never spoke of boys, or the future husband she hoped for. She'd become Matilda's study partner, then her confidante, then what the other girls had casually referred to as a Pash, someone with whom one "tried things out." Most girls, Matilda knew, stuck to learning to kiss. She'd soon grown used to hearing giggles from darkened corners. But Hanna was different; their first casual kisses had soon grown heated and confusing, and soon Matilda could think of little else than finding a few moments of privacy with the older girl and her soft, wandering hands.

Eventually, they'd begun sharing a bed for a few hours each night, and Hanna introduced Matilda to the bliss of having her nipples suckled and her cunt fondled until she was awash with pleasure. She'd been shy in return, but Hanna had encouraged her to experiment, and it had not taken them long to reach peaks of pleasure Matilda had never believed possible. Never had Matilda felt more powerful than when she'd coaxed Hanna to a shattering climax.

Neither of them had wept at their parting; too many people could see. But after, oh, Matilda had hidden herself in the school's dusty attic, sobs ripping out of her chest, heard by none but ancient trunks and a solitary dress form.

Had she never known Hanna, she might have been content with her lot. But in the years since, whenever she dropped her guard in the wee hours of the morning, she sorely felt the lack of intimacy, of physical pleasure, and of what she knew now might have become the depth of emotion such as a wife was meant to feel for her husband. The latter was usually the worst of it: it pained her greatly that she would never truly know love of that sort. But sometimes, sometimes, her longing for physical intimacy with another person was worse, an ache vivid as a toothache, for once experienced, it could not be undone or forgotten.

This long night, speaking intimacies with Cynthia in the dark, brought home to her how alone she'd been, and how alone she might continue to be if she allowed it. She wondered how the touch of Cynthia's hand would feel, on her bare skin. Was Cynthia's skin soft or roughened by work? Would her hand be warm, even in the night's chill?

Matilda had ceased speaking as she fell into her memories, and Cynthia had not pressed her; they traveled the pitted road in companionable silence, a silence that communicated...what, exactly? Perhaps all these intimate, erotic thoughts were only in her own mind. She could have been driven mad by loneliness and the stress of suddenly being here, in France, while a war raged. Shaking herself free of contemplation, she asked, "Is it always so quiet?"

Cynthia chuckled, low and warm. "You mean except for the ambulance banging along the potholes? It's not so quiet when my bus is loaded. The boys try to stay quiet, but they can't, always. I have to pretend I don't hear so they can hold onto their pride; they're just like my brothers sometimes, only politer. And during the day, well, there's a lot more shelling than we're getting right now."

"I meant a different sort of quiet. The quiet one feels when one is content—do you know the feeling I mean?"

"Am I happy doing this, you mean?" Cynthia spared her a glance, a shadowy movement of her head.

"Yes, I suppose. I'm...I find myself very content, just now. Content being here with you." Matilda clasped her hands together in her lap; she longed to reach out and touch Cynthia's arm.

"Me, too. It gets lonely sometimes. I'm used to it, you know. I spent a lot of my time alone with me and my horse and a couple of dogs. There's plenty of room for that in the desert. But this is nice. Real nice. There any of that coffee left?"

"I'm afraid I drank the rest of it."

"It's all right. That's why I gave it to you. I'm just a little sleepy is all. You mind if we stop for a bit? Just so I can sleep? Maybe a half hour. The doctors are always getting after me about driving when I'm too tired, and I don't want to wreck us."

There was really no choice in the matter. "I don't mind," Matilda said. "Will you be able to nap, in this cold?"

Cynthia slowed the ambulance, letting it rattle to a stop off the side of the road. "I was going to ask you," she said slowly, "if you'd mind us lying down in the back for a bit. There are some more blankets, and I could stretch out. It's really too cold for you to stay up here alone, and I wouldn't mind at all, but I don't want you to feel embarrassed."

"I wouldn't mind, either," Matilda said, adding daringly, "in fact, I would like that. I would like it very much. I've had a long day as well, and it would be a great comfort to me to sleep a little."

Cynthia was briefly silent, then she said, firmly, "Good. That's good."

They had to climb over the trunk full of telephone equipment. This proved impossible for Matilda in her snug skirt, until Cynthia offered to help her out of it, since "There's nobody here but us chickens."

This procedure was much less awkward than Matilda might have expected, though it felt odd to be partially disrobing by the side of a road. Beneath her skirt, her soft flannel knickers were much less constricting. It helped also that she wore a brassiere instead of a corset. Once the skirt was gone she could maneuver easily.

In the back of the ambulance, Matilda removed her hairpins and rested her head on her folded skirt. Cynthia pressed against her back, one arm draped over her waist, her chin atop Matilda's head. Several hospital blankets and Matilda's coat blocked the cold air, and soon their body heat mingled, multiplying the warmth. While the surface on which they lay was unforgiving, Matilda felt as if she could sink into the heat at her back and never emerge again. She could feel the faint softness of Cynthia's bosom through her shirtwaist. Cautiously, she laid her hand atop Cynthia's, where it curled into her waist. She could tell from the other woman's breathing that she was not yet asleep. "This is lovely. I wish we could stay this way forever," she murmured.

Cynthia chuckled into her hair. "I'd appreciate a mattress if you were wanting forever." She turned her hand over, lacing her fingers with Matilda's. Her fingers were calloused, her palm thrillingly rough. "We've been dancing around this all evening," she said, slow and easy. "At least, I've been scared to ask. I've been wondering if you might be a Sapphist."

Matilda flinched, her hand tightening on Cynthia's. She had never in her life said the word aloud. In dark moments, she'd scathingly thought of herself as an invert. "Yes," she whispered, then repeated, more loudly, "Yes. I think I am. And you?"

"Before I knew that fancy word," Cynthia confirmed. "I think I could be a real Disrupting Influence if I tried. I used to lie in my bed up in the attic and think on girls, and what I would do if I met one that liked me. But, I ought to tell you there was only one girl, outside of those stories I told myself. It was when I was taking the train from home, to get here. She was a Chicago girl, real pretty, and she asked me...well, I think that's private for now. I don't know if you think that's good or bad, that there was a girl."

Matilda was hard pressed not to turn over and stroke Cynthia's cheek in relief and fond affection. "Well, we both know what we're about, then. I had a friend in school, you see. For a few months. But that was long ago, and I am presently unattached."

Cynthia chuckled again. "You are so funny."

"I am?"

"You talk like a book." Before Matilda could retort, Cynthia had sat up, bending over her to press a soft kiss to her lips.

Matilda closed her eyes, savoring the touch. Then she parted her lips and sucked gently on Cynthia's lower lip, teasing with her tongue. She grasped the other woman's strong shoulders and pulled her down. They made a mess of the blankets while changing position to settle into each other, face to face this time. Cynthia's long limbs tangled in Matilda's petticoats while they kissed, slowly and teasingly. Daringly, Matilda scratched her nails through Cynthia's cropped hair, tugged on her earlobes, stroked her bare neck until her back arched, bringing their bosoms together with delicious pressure.

"Oh, that's good," Cynthia said, reaching down to fondle Matilda's breast through her shirtwaist. It buttoned up the front; soon she began to pop the buttons loose, nuzzling her way between them and rubbing her nose against Matilda's soft linen camisole. "You don't mind this? This is all right?"

"More," Matilda said, sliding her hands down to Cynthia's hips and gripping them firmly. "Put your leg over my hip. We haven't time to mess about, do we?"

"I want your skin," Cynthia said, yanking the camisole's hem free and shoving it up. She was stymied for a moment by the brassiere's hooks, but somehow got them loose, even in the dark.

Matilda burrowed her hands beneath Cynthia's wool jumper and the loose shirt beneath. "Oh, God," she said, finding no more layers. She covered small bare breasts and sighed at the silky feel of Cynthia's skin, then again as nipples hardened against her palms, sending stabs of wanting deep into her belly. A veil of restraint she hadn't even noticed lifted abruptly. "Let me," she said. "Let me."

"No, me first," Cynthia said. "I just got you out of all this." She swooped in close to nuzzle and suckle Matilda's breasts, rocking herself against Matilda's leg.

Being wanted like this made her feel giddy and powerful and desperate. Matilda grabbed Cynthia's hips, arching her back to give Cynthia better access. "More," she pleaded. "Press on my cunt with your hand."

"Not just yet," Cynthia said. Her tongue curled around Matilda's hardened nipple, then her lips closed on it. She suckled with slow pulls, until Matilda could scarcely bear the intensity.

"You—you like my breasts," she gasped.

"Oh, Jesus, yes," Cynthia said, switching to the other one, breaking off occasionally to speak. "You're so...so soft...and your hair is so pretty...and you just look...and sound...."

"You feel wonderful," Matilda said. She tangled her hands in Cynthia's thick hair, massaging her scalp and steering her to one breast or the other. When she could stand it no longer, she pushed her away, just a bit. "I am so close right now," Matilda said, her voice shaking. "I need your hand on me."

They bumped against the narrow bunks on either side of the ambulance, but somehow they managed to lie so Cynthia could ease her shaking hand into Matilda's damp knickers, caressing her mound and sliding effortlessly into the folds of her cunt. She didn't tease long; perhaps Matilda's rapid, panting breaths let her know something of Matilda's desperation.

For her part, Matilda burrowed her face in Cynthia's jumper, which she still wore. Each stroke of her cunt elicited a new agony of desire, until Cynthia's fingers skidded, hard, over her clit and began a rapid massage. She lost all consciousness of anything but need, reaching and reaching for a depth of pleasure she hadn't felt in far too long, until suddenly she was flung into her climax and past it, and left trembling and panting against Cynthia's throat.

They lay for a long time in silence broken only by their harsh breathing. Matilda fumbled in the dark until she could lay her hand against Cynthia's cheek. "I would like to help you climax," she said. "Will you allow it?"

"Jesus, you can do anything to me if you just say it like that," Cynthia mumbled. "But after that I really do need to sleep a little, that wasn't just an excuse to get you out of your skirt."

Matilda laughed. "Oh, my dear." She struggled up, planting one hand to either side of Cynthia's head. "Push up your jumper for me. And your shirt."

"Yes, ma'am."

"Do you like having your breasts touched?"

"It seems I—oh, Jesus—I do."

"I can tell. Can you take over for me? I want to use my mouth on your cunt."

"Jesus. Yes. I—I can do that."

"Good girl." Matilda found Cynthia's trouser buttons and slipped them free, one by one. "Lift your rear for me, just for a moment, so I can get these out of the way."

"Yes, ma'am."

"I like how polite you are." Matilda pulled Cynthia's knickers down as well, and wished she had enough light to see her in her full glory. She would enjoy seeing every soft, slick fold; she made do with tracing Cynthia's cunt with a fingertip.

"Don't know...why I'm...doing it. You ain't my teacher."

"Feel free to keep on, I don't mind in the least." Matilda bent to nuzzle Cynthia's lower belly, and the crease where her thighs met her torso, and finally her cunt. "Are you touching your breasts?"

"Yes, ma'am." The honorific ended in a gasp as Matilda peeled open Cynthia's soft folds and began exploring with her tongue. The air was rich with their mingled scents and warmth; the distant thunder of bombs seemed mere background as Matilda searched out the places and pressures that caused Cynthia to twist and moan and beg loudly, music to Matilda's ears. It was deliciously freeing.

She wasn't sure how long she licked and tasted, but she wanted it to last forever. Cynthia would probably appreciate a more prompt crisis, however, so when Matilda felt hands in her hair, tight and desperate, she shifted to rapid movements of her fingers and the regular pressure of her teeth on Cynthia's clit.

"Almost—" Cynthia said.

Matilda placed her hand where her mouth had been, and rubbed. "Come for me, my dear."

Cynthia obeyed. Matilda held her close while she shook and cried out in the aftershocks, kissing her softly as she drifted off to sleep. Matilda didn't know what the future might hold for them, but...that would be the adventure, wouldn't it? They would complete the delivery of the trunk (oh blessed trunk, that had provided a bed for their intimacy), and then...and then.

Those were dreams. What would truly happen, when the dawn came?

Matilda lay awake for a long time, listening to the distant crash of shells. Men would be left bleeding after each concussion. Cynthia and her ambulance would bear their torn bodies to hospitals, where some of them would die, leaving sisters and wives and children and parents behind to grieve. And the next day, she would do it again, and again. She was strong, and would remain strong in her duty, in saving the lives of others for themselves and for their loved ones.

Tomorrow, though, they would deliver the telephone

equipment. Matilda would assemble it and test its functions; she would likely need to train some few soldiers or VADs or French workers in its use, if there was no one else to do so. It might take a few days. She would need to contact her sister-in-law somehow, to let her know what had happened, and why she would be delayed in returning. She could have a few more stolen days with Cynthia, if their duties permitted.

And after that? She didn't know. Was there a place for her here, in the war zone? Would the war ever end? If it did, what then? What might America be like, for a woman such as her? Would Cynthia want that?

She needed to sleep. Matilda pressed her lips to Cynthia's temple. She wanted more than just this one night, but for now, she would cling to each moment as if it might be her last. Fate had delivered her to Cynthia, and for now that would have to be enough.

EAGLE OF DEATH, RAVEN OF WAR

BY JESSICA TAYLOR

1917: WWI: Russia

The first time I made love to Maria Bochkareva we shared a cigarette I rolled for us afterward. It was a small gift, a replacement for the many offerings I wanted to bestow. The thin paper was crusted with bits of mud. We passed it back and forth as we lay shoulder to shoulder in her green tent issued by the Imperial Russian Empire.

As I sit on a wooden stool in the depths of a trench on our Western Front, I recall my progression to the warrior I am now. I wait for the evening to pass into night, so I can go to Commander Bochkareva and show her all I have learned beneath her.

The Russian Empire dissolved months ago after Tsar Nicholas abdicated, and the infantile government of the Russian Republic was delivered 15 March 1917. It had been a war within a war for Russia: first the war with the world tore into us, and then our own revolutions leached us. The country's devastated resources remained the same whether we had a king or a president.

Our battalion, the 1st Russian Women's Battalion of Death, had its training camp outside Petrograd. Some women still called our city Saint Petersburg, but I grew up with the beautiful word Petrograd gliding easily from my tongue.

My first time with the Commander, I'd needed her help—and she'd known it. She'd pronounced to the Battalion of Death that we would deploy to the trenches in the west to make a push against the Germans.

Though I'd lived in war for most of my adult life, I'd never been threatened in Petrograd. After the Commander's announcement, I was weakened by thoughts of my death. I was overcome with insomnia when I tried to sleep that night. My heart pounded rapidly, like the eagle on the old Imperial flag. I felt vertiginous and close to sobbing as I stumbled past the Commander's huge hobbled mare on my way to her quarters.

Entering her musky tent in the still night, I was surprised at the hung bouquets of dill and poppy spicing its interior. Commander Bochkareva's quarters seemed a palace compared to mine, as large as my *babushka*'s walk-in root cellar stuffed full of beets and potatoes.

Uninvited, it was presumptuous and almost disobedient to throw back the flap of her tent without permission, but she didn't seem offended by my presence when she looked up at me. My brown hair straggled over my shoulders and my chest heaved with waves of hyperventilation.

The Commander was awake, sitting at a small wooden table, playing cards with herself. Surrounding her were scribbled maps of our infested western borders. Her black hair was twisted into a murky green kerchief and her blue eyes glowed by the light of her oil lantern.

"Lilya," she addressed me informally. "How can I help you?" She lay down her yellowed cards.

My wool trousers were scratchy against my sweaty body. I sat on the ground next to her with my legs crossed as she soothed me with stories of our brave sisters in battle. Eventually, my heart slowed. A seed of courage had begun, inspired by her tales and her calmness.

"Tell me why you wanted to fight, Lilya."

"Because I love our home."

"Tell my why you followed me to the Battalion of Death."

"Because I wanted to be as strong as you. I wanted to fight like you for the motherland."

But there was also another reason, one I didn't dare speak aloud. The iron curves of her body fortified by her dedication to Russia were the most attractive things I had ever witnessed. I wanted to defend Russia like her, but I also longed to know her. What lay beneath her uniform? I wanted to discover the body beneath all that wool.

Maria Bochkareva's voice softened. "Is there any other reason you came here?"

I nodded my head, my lower lip beginning to blush and beat like a heart. I still wasn't able to speak it, but I thought to myself, *Perhaps there is also something for me to give to her.*

I was sitting on the canvas floor below her, and my head drifted to the side and unintentionally rested on her thigh. My cheek pulsed red. I wondered what her skin might smell like. She didn't take this move as a sign of cowardice. Instead, she worked her hand into the roots of my hair. The tips of her fingers were rounded and callused.

My body felt suddenly awake in a new way, and I twitched with longing between my legs.

Then the Commander took over. "Sit next to me."

I obeyed and elevated myself to the wooden bench.

Soothing my need, she touched me first. Faded freckles littered my nose, and she softly drew a finger over them, as though their minuscule topography meant something special to her. My skin burned beneath her touch. Since the first time I'd seen her a month before, as she campaigned through Petrograd collecting women for her Battalion of Death, I knew she would change my life.

"Unbutton," she exhaled.

Though I felt shy, it became easy under her instruction. When I shed my blouse, the chilly air calmed me. I hadn't undressed for anyone but my husband, now dead, on our wedding night a year earlier when I was still eighteen. Certainly my skin hadn't glowed beneath his touch. As I wondered what the breasts of a woman a decade my elder looked like, I grew wet and licked my lips with anticipation.

She released her thick black hair from its cap and the smell of oil and herbs engulfed me. A few pins flashed in the light of the lantern as they dropped to the ground. Her hair fell in clumped waves, reminding me of the calm but swift Neva River flowing through our city. Each summer when I lifted my skirts to dip a foot into its waters, it always soothed my hot body.

Before the Commander kissed me for first time, she leaned in to my ear and whispered her demand. "Call me Yasha when we're alone."

Her lips finally alighted on mine. She smoothed her rough hands over my nipples, which made me inhale with surprise and then exhale with a moan of pleasure.

"Stand." When I did, she arose with me.

She undressed herself and my eyes widened as she undid first her blouse and then her trousers. Perhaps she knew I'd fumble her buttons. Beneath the Imperial issue uniform sewn over with the badges of the Republic, she was nude and breathtaking.

Yasha's hair streamed over her clavicles. Her breasts were firm and still proud, like mine. Even by the light of the lantern, I could see the burgundy of their hard tips. My own nipples became tight in response and begged to be caressed. I closed my eyes at the sensation, but made myself open them so I could see the rest of her.

A hollow extended from the base of her throat and down her chest, then continued over her abdomen. The contours of her ridged belly muscles took my breath away. Her hips were square and strong, with round thighs that I knew could march for miles. Her feet were small; I wanted to bow and kiss their creamy arches before I arose to her inner thighs, but I was too shy to initiate.

"Touch yourself, Lilya."

I had always wanted to lay my hand over the soft skin that sometimes ached in the middle of the night, calling for me to rub and stroke it, but I'd never had the courage to do so. Finally, with my Commander directing me, I was empowered.

As I rubbed slow circles over myself, Yasha watched me. She had the same look of pleasure and dedication on her face that I had seen watching her demonstrations of bayonet work or marksmanship. My nipples were tight in the cool air and my center grew warmer and warmer beneath my fingers and her hazy stare. I gazed at her and grew wetter than I'd ever been, until she finally walked forward to me.

As our breasts brushed against one another, she set a foot onto her wooden cot. She grabbed my wrist, pushed my hand between her legs, pressed a finger over mine and showed me how to please her. Then she pushed fingers inside my wetness and massaged my clitoris with her thumb at the same time. My muscles became tight as clockwork; my body felt like a river ready to crush a dam, and then thunder spread through my body and lightning overtook me. As I cried out into the night, confused but utterly pacified, she chuckled in my ear and placed a hand softly over my mouth.

"Shh...Lilya. Shh," she cooed to me.

When I brought her to climax, she exhibited control of her breath to disguise her moans. As we fell together onto the green cot that night, I proffered the tobacco, but I hardly let her smoke it. She'd inhale from the dirty bone. Then I'd take the cigarette and kiss where it had been, sliding my tongue softly over her lips before I entered her mouth. Over and over I did this, hungry for the taste of her mouth and the wetness of her tongue.

For a week before we left for the trenches, we went through this ritual. I stole into her palace at night. She told me stories of bravery, implying my capacity for such heroism. She named me her Raven of War, and I called her my Eagle of Death. Then we made love by the light of her oil lamp.

One week ago, the 1st Russian Women's Battalion of Death came to the front. The trenches outside the city of Smorgon are now deep scars in the land of the mother. Though it's July, the ground is still cool when I pace, awaiting news of who will come to help us in this battle. There's been word of Romanian assistance. All I see though is our soldiers falling back, and no one but us women from Petrograd have arrived within the last few weeks.

Not a single woman of our three hundred has fled despite the rat infestations, the lack of food, and the broken Russian men mewling for vodka. Not one of us has shuddered at the intermittent rattle of machine guns that litter the day and night.

The poorly bandaged men plastered along the sides of the trenches talk at me like a broken phonograph. *Girl,* they spit at my feet. *Go home to your husband.* My chin as high as the Commander's, I tell them every time, *He's dead. And those are not my orders.*

Today, we received Commander Bochkareva's new directive as the dull sun hung mid-sky. It was dark though in that cleared bunker where she addressed us.

"My sisters," she boomed. Her boots were shined and she wore full decoration. "We've received orders from Minister Kerensky and General Brusilov that it's our time to push through and rid our lands of the Germans."

"We fly forward tomorrow at dawn, over the lip of the trench. With courage and true hearts, I know you will soar with me to honor our mother Russia."

Though I didn't feel excitement at the prospect of my own death or those of my fellow soldiers, I didn't feel fear at these words. The breathing of my sisters around me synchronized. A feeling of trust emanated into the room as we listened to Commander Bochkareva.

Since arriving at the trenches, I haven't spent any nights with Yasha. I don't think she's slept much. I lie in my cot each night though and mimic the motion of her hands on me until I feel the speed of my climax. Her scent floats about me as I reverberate with pleasure. The memory of her cool blue eyes first ignites and then cools my body. Each time I imagine her hands on me, my toes curl and I control my breath the way she's taught me.

I realized that tonight I must find her, for it may be my last night to honor her. With a cup of fresh water from our low stock, I cleaned myself as best I could. The water made me think of the river back in Petrograd. Perhaps, I thought, Yasha and I could stroll next to it one day, the sun kissing our lips and cheeks as we walk side by side. I pulled fingers through my long brown hair and set it up beneath my hat. *What would itbe like to comb through Yasha's every night as we prepared for bed?*

I shined my boots until they grew bright as Yasha's eyes. I pulled my full-length green coat over my nakedness. As it settled, my skin tingled with anticipation of Yasha's touch. I slung my rifle over my shoulder, because I go nowhere without it these days.

Now I rest on the wooden stool outside my bunker. Following my reverie, I watch the sky go first pink, and then orange, and finally navy as the sun sinks from this side of the destroyed world. Behind me is war, and before me it continues through many languages, countrysides, and capitals. In the morning, it will be my time to go forward into it. But now, it is time to find Yasha.

As I begin my trek to her, bats take flight above me and the smell of stewed cabbage comes from either our trench or theirs. I find the Commander as I have before. She's alone in a bunker, playing cards at a wooden table. The maps have been put away, the trenches long since memorized.

"Lilya," she greets me. "You look well, and prepared." She nods to my spotless boots.

There is a makeshift door over the opening to her quarters. I close it behind me and lay my rifle in front of it. I salute her.

"Commander Bochkareva, I come to give you my gratitude before we go over the top. You didn't just teach me to shoot a rifle, you taught me how to hit my mark. You didn't just teach me how to drop a man to the ground with my weight, you also taught me five ways to break his shooting arm."

Now that I have thanked the Commander, it's time to honor Yasha. My sex is already beginning to awaken and dampen. I can hardly wait for her hair to spill out from under her hat.

Her eyes are more hollowed than I have seen them before, and the bottom of her grey blouse hangs out of her trousers. I hope to give her a moment of respite, allow her to sleep a few hours of this night that we wait.

Yasha slides a foot out, relaxing back into her chair. She lays down her cards: four aces.

I drop the hand I raised to my brow for the Commander. One metal button at a time, I undo my jacket to begin my new salute to Yasha. I look her in the eyes, whereas before I might have averted my gaze.

When I reach her, the lapels of my jacket swing to the side and brush my breasts. One pink, erect nipple peeks out. The pale skin of my knee contrasts against my black boot. I can already smell the excitement emanating from under my dark splash of hair.

Setting my hands on my hips, I tower over her. "Stand up, Yasha." My voice is brave.

She stands, an inch at a time, her eyes on my round breasts that are almost replicas of hers. Her clothes caress over the sections of my body that are exposed. The friction makes me want her hands on me, but this time isn't for me.

I pull the hat from her head, revealing the clean black hair before it becomes crusted with battle. I comb my hands through it, and rest my thumbs at Yasha's temples. Her neck relaxes from my massage. Sliding my hands down to her cheeks, I cup her face in my palm.

I lean in to whisper in her ear. "Yasha, you are my Eagle of Death."

Her forehead drifts forward to rest on mine. We sway together, as if music is playing for us. Her eyes crease at the sides when she says, "And you are my Raven of War."

With this she closes her eyes and rumbles a groan. I bring my lips to hers and kiss her deeply. She has to understand me, and what I've become because of her.

Without trembling, a certainty weeks before, I undo her blouse and slide it from her shoulders. Her breasts are bared to me. I stare, transfixed, pulsing and throbbing at their sight. I kiss down the bone in the center of her chest, beginning at the hollow in the base of her throat. I lay a slow kiss at the end of each nipple, loving the feel of their hardness on my tongue. And then I rub my thumbs over and over as Yasha relaxes even more before me, whimpers escaping her lips. If she allows herself these sounds of weakness, she must understand my desire to share her burdens tonight.

I kiss her mouth again while I remove her trousers. They

scrape both of our legs as they fall to the dirt ground. Her cot is behind us. I remove my jacket and lay it down to give my queen the comfort she deserves.

"Lilya, my Raven," she says as she moves behind me, encircling my waist with her arms. We sway for a moment together, still safe as a burst of machine-gun fire ruptures the stillness between trenches. This happens, for no reason, from time to time. In the morning, though, it will mean something.

She kisses the bones down my spine. "I worry for you tomorrow, sweet girl."

I turn around to her. "I can do nothing but fly because you have taught me. Let me show you."

Guiding her to the cot, I go to my knees before her. I spread her legs, caressing their tense muscles, and slide my tongue up the length of one. Her black hair glistens at her center. She's already wet when I bring my tongue to her, and her clitoris tastes rich as butter.

Above me, Yasha is letting go. She is sinking into me, rocking against me.

Just before she is about to break, I remove my mouth. I get up from the ground and hang over her. I slide my bent thigh against her sex as I let her buck onto it. It glides easily, her slick juices coating my leg. I worship each breast, caressing the firm tissue as she continues her movement. I love the feel of her rough hair abrading my leg as I suck at the ridges of each nipple.

Then I flip her onto her hands and knees. Behind her, I draw her back toward me by the hips. I sink my tongue into her wet center and let her ride it as I massage circles into her.

She is close to erupting, the sounds of her pleasure flowing from her mouth as if she is telling the world of her joy and her sorrow. I remove my mouth and nip each of her strong buttocks. She is so lovely from behind as I push my fingers into her while I stroke her clitoris. I feel myself go into a trance, my mouth half open and my eyes glued to her opening. I push down into her soft walls, thanking her with each stroke.

As the thunder of her climax pours over me, my own body tenses as if I will also release along with her. I hope she has heard me: *thank you, Yasha, my Commander and my Eagle.*

I hold her in my arms after, as she once did for me. I rock her and run my hands through her hair. I roll us a cigarette that we pass back and forth as we lie shoulder to shoulder. Finally, she drifts off to sleep in my arms, and I feel that I have done the last thing I needed to do before we fly over the top.

Eventually, the sun creeps slowly into the sky and mutes the shining stars that lit the night. The dawn breaks blood red, the color of Russia. *Let this be an omen in our favor,* I pray to myself. Beneath me, the Eagle stirs.

"Are you ready my Raven?" The Commander is pulling on pants and boots.

I stand next to her. We embrace one last long moment before I leave for my bunker to dress for war.

She presses a hand onto my cheek. "You are brave, Lilya. I will see you on the other side."

"I fly where you fly."

THE BATTLE OF BLAIR MOUNTAIN

BY DENA HANKINS

1921: The Battle of Blair Mountain: West Virginia

SueLynn shifted her rifle off her collarbone and climbed the hill with the agility of long practice. This wasn't her mountain, but it was her mountain range. She knew how to move over ground covered with leaves, springy and rotting and full of life. She headed for a rock outcropping to see the next holler.

SueLynn wore boots and britches like the men, shot game and cussed and drank like the men too. When they had limped home after the Great War, they hadn't been too terribly surprised to hear told she'd gone down in the mines while they were away.

She leaned against the rock, scanning the holler and the hill beyond for Chafin's gun-thug deputies.

Only days before, the miners had been heading on home like Bill Blizzard said, though he was no coward and wanted to fight. With the President himself sending federals against them, well, it looked like Logan and Mingo Counties weren't getting unionized just then.

Sheriff Chafin couldn't let well enough alone. He'd put together his private army, 2000 men strong, and couldn't bear losing the chance to kill him some unionizers. Those demon-spawn started shooting union sympathizers up in Sharples, catching families in the crossfire. SueLynn and 10,000 fellow miners had turned back to fight.

Thinking on it, SueLynn's purpose flipped from hiding to hunting. Her sharp vision had been a boon to the family when rationing had near to starved them during the war and her kills had fed the lot.

She kept behind the rock, but her finger itched to shoot the sold-out bastards who beat and killed folks for wanting to be safer at their dangerous work, for wanting legal tender and not the trap of company script in a company house in a company town.

Dozens of men straggled over the side of the hill, arraying themselves along the ridge so they could provide a fusillade in case of enemy action. Sunlight bounced from hill to hill, skipping the holler below. A gleam from the river battled the early dark, peeking from between tree branches.

Some of the men come back from Europe did their fair share of bragging, telling stories on themselves, making themselves out to be heroes. Mostly the men SueLynn wanted at her back were the ones who shut that talk down. The ones who picked up their guns, knowing they may be shooting at folks, with sober and careful thought. Not the braggarts and not the odd ones, 'cause the Lord knew plenty came back half out of the world, barely making do for themselves.

Word came along they were to bed down behind the ridge. They'd be up and through the holler before dawn so they could attack from above, sun behind their backs, while the gun thugs were wiping the sleep from their decadent eyes.

SueLynn didn't give a hoot for military tactics. There were folks better qualified than her to figure on when and where they'd throw down with the company men. She quivered in a surge of excitement, like a horse at a starting line. She'd learned plenty about herself since the miners had started unionizing West Virginia, but she'd never imagined such a rush from the prospect of pitched battle.

She didn't feel the need to bed down in secret, nor did she buttress herself with men known to her to be safe. She went about her business like any other miner. She'd learnt who she really was while the men were away at war, and she wouldn't compromise her freedom by hemming it in for safety's sake.

Barring one personal duty too intimate to carry out among the men.

She slipped out of her pack and left it leaning against the warm rock. She didn't leave her rifle, not being a fool.

Men covered the shadowed side of the mountain, so she slipped across to the sunny side to do her business. A couple hundred yards beyond the ridge, she found a likely log and shucked her pants down around her ankles to piss.

Holding her rifle in one hand and pulling her britches forward with the other, most of her weight rested against the log at her back. The bark pulled at her flannel shirt, which she'd purchased out of her own hard-earned script. The ground cover soaked up the stream without a splash and the smell of piss faded fast.

She splashed herself with a little water from her canteen and stood to put her clothing aright. A snapping branch stopped her hands. She turned her head slowly, eyes scanning, ears tuning in like the radios she'd heard tell of.

Without a whisper of sound, SueLynn buttoned her pants and raised her rifle from the ground. She shouldered the butt and laid her finger beside the trigger. More worried about shooting a friend than not shooting an enemy, she pointed the barrel at the ground and crept across the small clearing to the next fallen tree.

A pleased groan followed hard on the sound of water hitting the ground. The smell hit her next. Someone else was out for a private piss. She stood, holding tight to the rifle until she knew who was over the other side of the half-rotted tree trunk.

The person there would have to be very short of stature since the tree wasn't big enough to hide a regular person standing to piss, but a brown head wavered up before she could puzzle it out.

Several facts hit her one after another. A man squats to shit, not to piss, but she'd heard nothing but water and sniffing presented nothing much to her nose.

"Who goes there?" She spoke fast.

"Hell," said the other person, with a jerk and stumble. "You scart the piss out of me."

SueLynn had to laugh. "That's hard to believe. You must have been empty with all that moaning and groaning you were doing." The person flushed and fumbled at their clothing. SueLynn still couldn't credit what she'd discovered and she asked her question with all the righteousness of someone with lots of nosy family. "Are you a woman or a man?"

The stranger's narrowed eyes and defensive stance told SueLynn how things stood.

"I'm a woman too, in case you can't tell. SueLynn Harmon from outside Marmet. Who are your people?"

"Tanners, out of Little Coal River."

"Well, Miz Tanner, your people sure did light some dynamite under the county troopers."

"Tanner'll do. We got our licks in."

"Captured and disarmed Chafin's troopers and sent them packing. I'd say you did okay."

Tanner shrugged like it weren't nothing, but she flushed a little. "They crossed us more than we could stand. Thought the union would never take hold down here, but they made it where there's nothing to do but go down in the hole. Push come to shove, we got war in Bloody Mingo and ain't nothing to do about it but fight."

SueLynn got to talking, easy-like, to set Tanner's mind to rest. "For me the union's about taking care of folks. It's a damn shame when a person can't care for those they care about. You go down in the mines?" Tanner nodded, flat-mouthed. "I can't claim to love mining, but I love making an independent living and I'm not smart as my sister. She's a teacher."

Tanner slapped her hat against her thigh. "For my part, I prefer striking to mining."

SueLynn laughed again. Better. "Doesn't seem much safer to me, and living under canvas gets old. I go stay with my sister now and then, when it gets to me some. Good food and town folk to talk to. My daddy was with the Wobblies, back when it meant something. One big union." Tanner nodded, silent. "I don't know about these new unions. Any union keeps us women out ain't a union. It's a goddamn club."

Tanner kept her silence and SueLynn wondered at her thoughts. Few enough women worked the mines and even fewer made any effort to keep their jobs after the men came back. SueLynn knew why she did it, but Tanner was a tough nut.

"Well, come along back and we'll get some chuck."

Tanner hesitated. "My family don't know I'm out here."

"You snuck along for the fight?" SueLynn appreciated a woman with bottom. "What say I get some hot food for us both and we spread our bedrolls down here a ways?"

Tanner looked her in the eye for the first time and SueLynn just about squeaked. Tanner was pretty as a boy, all sweet lips and long eyelashes catching the setting sun. It wasn't the first time she'd gotten herself turned around, feeling warm about a woman the way her sister was about her beaus. When Tanner spoke, simply to say "thanks," SueLynn saw her tongue flash between her teeth and felt that same quivering excitement as before.

"I'll be back soon as I can," SueLynn stuttered out. She crossed the clearing and hopped the tree trunk before she could give it another thought. She went back up to her pack and got out her bowl, shouldered the pack and followed her nose to the cookpot.

She slopped beans in her bowl and took a few quick mouthfuls. Filling it back up, she rushed back to her new friend, hoping all the time that Tanner would still be at the clearing. She did act awful skittish. When she jumped the tree trunk for a third time, Tanner was on the other side, kneeling on her bedroll with her rifle in her hand and a stick in her mouth.

"Just me. Don't shoot." SueLynn tried to make like she was joking, but the gun had given her a fright. Not from fearing Tanner, but from realizing she'd forgot all about the possibility of running into Sheriff Chafin's gun thugs and hired killers. She swallowed dry and assured herself they wouldn't say boo without heavy artillery backing their play.

She put the bowl on Tanner's blanket.

"Union ain't against women." Tanner put her gun down and sat.

"That your experience? Eat up."

"Mother Jones been all over this country."

Tanner pulled a spoon from her near-empty pack. "I'd like to see more than a hill and a holler."

"Mother Jones wants us to turn back. She lost her nerve."

Tanner stiffened. "She's old. Eighty, maybe ninety years old. She knows how many die in a thing like this."

SueLynn let that settle in while Tanner ate like she was starving. She'd thought a lot more about killing than dying.

Tanner went on after she'd cleaned the bowl with her finger and licked the gravy off. "It's like she says. We just equipment to them. Don't make no nevermind how much coal you load or how long your kin lived on the land. You stand alone, you're just so much trash to these people."

"You're a regular organizer, ain't you? You with your pierced ears and boy clothes." SueLynn unstrapped her bedroll and sat on it without laying it out. She put her elbows on her knees and watched Tanner's expression move from the fervor of a believer to the sourness of a sufferer.

Tanner's mouth twisted. "I was fifteen when my pop went down and never come back. I was just a regular girl putting up blackberries when they came to tell me. Spraying the walls down cost too much so coal dust caught fire, dynamite blew. Took two days to find them and couldn't tell who was who when they brung them out." SueLynn kept silent out of respect for the miners, killed by cheap operators. "I was on my own. After a while having no luck getting game, I gave in. Trapper boy, section three. Superintendent says he won't let one union man step foot in his coal mine. What about me, I say?"

"Pointing out I'm a woman never did me a lick of good on the job."

"Got me a fist in the eye for my trouble. Ever since, I been pretending to be a man so hard I almost forget I'm not." Tanner picked her stick back up and started cleaning her teeth. "Sassafras?"

SueLynn said, "Sure, I'll take a stick. Don't sound like you're happy as a miner, or as a man." Tanner pulled another sassafras stick from her pack and SueLynn chewed the end to soften it.

"Sometimes you got to bend so you don't break."

SueLynn nodded meditatively. "Folks give me space. I don't

pretend to be a man and I don't put on womanly airs to satisfy my kin. I'm something else of my own. Guess they're used to me by now." Wanting to open up to Tanner, she made a dangerous joke on herself. "It'd be different if I messed around with men behind their wives' backs, but I'm more likely to get caught with my hand up a petticoat than down some britches."

A whine grew in her ears and she looked around. Tanner reached for her rifle so fast SueLynn dropped the sassafras stick and jumped for hers before she recognized the sound.

"Hellfire and damnation. Army Marin MB-1 bombers. Courtesy of the president, I read."

Tanner crouched, alert as a dog on the scent. "I thought they was renting out private planes."

Just then, the bomb bay doors opened. "Holy shit, they're coming our way."

SueLynn gasped at the sight of a speck falling from the airplane, then another and another. Munitions left over from the Great War screamed down along the ridge and SueLynn flashed on all the men staggered down that way. She jumped to her feet and started running, but she landed hard on the ground when Tanner sprang at her and pinned her down.

"You can't save them by running toward the bombs, you idiot. We got to hunker down under cover. Long as they don't see us, they won't aim for us."

SueLynn planted a foot and heaved her hip to flip Tanner over. She kept rolling because Tanner was right. There was no defense against death from the sky.

She came to rest near some scrub and shimmied under. She brought her rifle, in case of follow-up attack. Tanner whisked her bedding away from the clearing and scurried back so fast her blankets flapped behind her.

The airplane's engines got loud and SueLynn's stomach jumped. "Get your ass down here." SueLynn hoped the growl hid the shake in her voice.

"Wrap up in the blanket. It'll be harder to see us if we're covered up."

SueLynn pulled the blanket over them both while Tanner slipped under the bushes next to her. She poked herself with a branch and had an idea. "Help me tuck the blanket between the branches. Keep it off our faces and give us some air."

Tanner moved to help and elbowed SueLynn in the tit. "Shit, I'm sorry."

"Don't worry about it now. I'll get you back later." SueLynn grinned when Tanner choked on a shaky laugh. She put her hand on Tanner's shoulder and pushed her flat on her back. "I think we're good."

Tanner closed her eyes and moved her head back and forth on the leaves. "Why haven't they exploded yet?"

SueLynn sighed. "Rumor is they're homemade bombs and some are duds. If the president sent bombs with the bombers, that's worse by far. They'll turn you to hamburger."

The shudder that passed through Tanner made SueLynn regret her loose tongue.

She rolled up on her side and looked down at Tanner. "Hey, I'm sorry. I didn't mean it."

Hard on her words came the first thud. SueLynn didn't want to imagine where it had hit. When the second bomb went off, she grabbed Tanner's hand. "Lord let us see the end of this." Two more bombs, close enough now to hear them whomp and reverberate in the holler.

Tanner pulled SueLynn's hand across her belly and SueLynn swallowed hard. "I can't stand the waiting. They're trying to drive us crazy." Tanner jerked under SueLynn's hand when the next bomb went off.

"We'll stay close and keep each other calm."

"I'm not a kid. And I saw you looking at me."

SueLynn went to stone. "What are you talking about?"

"Don't act the lamb with me. You wanted to kiss me and then you run off."

Dynamite couldn't have shaken SueLynn harder. "Leave me be."

"You ever kissed a girl?" Tanner grabbed her shoulder when SueLynn tried to turn away. "I have. I kissed a boy too, but right now, I want to kiss a woman."

"You got some nerve, kid." That's all SueLynn could say before her mouth pushed hard on Tanner's. She'd had no intention of doing it, but she kept her lips where she'd put them. Eyes open, she could see the flush mount across Tanner's cheeks. She had some cockamamie notion of making Tanner push her away, but that's not what happened.

The next explosion hit close enough to put her reticence to rest. The impact rumbled through the ground. Fear weakened her muscles and strengthened her will.

She leaned over Tanner, bringing their bodies close. Tanner quivered and she slid right on top. The press of their lips turned into a slide. Tanner opened her mouth and SueLynn fell inside.

Hard and slick. Tanner's clean teeth and between them the tongue she'd glimpsed earlier. Soft and strong, thick and rough on top, flavored with the sassafras she'd been chewing. SueLynn filled Tanner's mouth and had hers filled in turn.

An ear-pounding blast shook the tree and leaves fell on the blanket above them. SueLynn jumped at the small pain of Tanner's teeth on her bottom lip. The fear and the anger at being made to fear spurred her to grab Tanner's shoulders and push her harder into the ground. She shoved downward with her hips into Tanner's and their legs slipped into a tangle.

Her thigh is between my legs. SueLynn saw the words, heard them as though they were read aloud. She pushed her torso up to get more contact, harder, and felt Tanner's hands slide up her ribs and between her arms to her front. To her tits.

Tanner undulated under her, squeezing her tits and groping for her nipples. When she found them, Tanner opened her eyes.

Tanner's flush covered her face and neck. Her eyes gleamed in the dimness under the concealing blanket and her lips pressed together in a hum. When they opened on a moan, SueLynn groaned along with her.

She had to ask. "Do you know what we're about?"

"Pleasing each other, I expect."

No better answer than that. SueLynn dove for Tanner's neck, the dirt and sweat only making her more real. She'd done things with friends, naked at the swimming hole and wearing nightgowns in a tent behind the house. They'd all smelled like soap and tasted like it too. Tanner tasted like honest work and sassafras. Her head fell back and offered the heat behind her ear to SueLynn's mouth.

Desperate to find all the secret places where Tanner's essence would condense and linger, SueLynn pulled back again. Tanner rose to capture her mouth and SueLynn groaned. The sound soaked into the silence and they both stilled.

"Do you think they're done?" SueLynn listened for clues. No birds. Nothing moved outside their blanket-tent. Tanner shifted below her and SueLynn couldn't control the jerk of her hips. She laughed roughly. "Hold still, baby. I can't think when you do that."

Tanner reached up and touched her face with her fingertips. She stroked down SueLynn's cheek, over her jaw, and down her neck to the buttons on her thick shirt. "We'll live or we'll die, but won't be the mine that takes our lives if we end right here, right now. If I'm the first person in three generations to die above ground, I'll consider myself lucky."

SueLynn shuddered. She wasn't sure whether it was Tanner's resigned talk of dying or the clever fingers that exposed her undershirt and then pushed beneath to stroke the top of her tit. SueLynn wouldn't accept a hopeless, meaningless death. She'd fight for life with every tool and weapon she could bring to hand.

SueLynn pulled her thigh from the heat between Tanner's legs and straddled her waist. She clamped her knees tight around the narrowing above hard hip bones. She slipped her suspenders down her arms, finished unbuttoning her flannel, and dropped it aside. She shucked off her cotton undershirt and Tanner's cool, dry hands followed the hem as it rose. Tanner slid her hands over SueLynn's round belly and never hesitated, sweeping up under the slight hang of her tits, then around the sensitive sides. SueLynn's nipples puckered in the cool air and Tanner stared.

Tanner made small, soothing motions down the outside curve of SueLynn's tits until SueLynn grabbed her hands and pressed them hard against her nipples. Tanner squeezed and SueLynn's belly jumped. The weightlessness, the pressure felt so good she thought she was queasy, only recognizing the truth when she grabbed Tanner's face and made her look at her.

She'd explored feeling good, used her hands and sometimes a pillow to rub on. She'd rubbed on other girls and been awed by their abandoned pleasure. What Tanner made her feel with fingertips and palms was closer to the end than the beginning. She felt ready to come right out of her skin already.

She went to work, fast and unsteady, on the buttons hiding Tanner's body, leaning down for a quick kiss, too hungry, too desperate for Tanner to join her. Tanner thrust her hips up, unbalancing SueLynn so that she fell forward and guiding her tumble to get at her nipple.

Tanner closed her teeth around it and SueLynn made a sound she didn't recognize. Too used to stifling her pleasure, the open-mouthed, high-pitched cry brought a moment of self-consciousness. She looked down at Tanner's hair, her brow, and her nose buried in SueLynn's own flesh. If she were naked, she would have climbed Tanner's body and put her most private, most tender flesh right over her mouth and chin and nose.

"Will you use your mouth on me, Tanner?" She ground the words out, driving spikes from her nipple to her womb. Her guts pulled and shifted, leaving an opening that she desperately wanted Tanner to enter.

"I want to see you." Tanner tugged at the blanket that further dimmed the waning light.

"Do you think we're safe?" SueLynn didn't want to give up their slight protection if the airplanes were coming back.

"Those people don't want to be in the air after dark. They're done throwing explosives at us for now."

SueLynn sat back up and tugged the blanket free of the branches. She stood and spread it beside them. Tanner put a hand up and SueLynn wished she could freeze time. Tanner's short, dark hair was mussed from her fingers and her neck showed livid red where SueLynn had bit and sucked at her. The half-open shirt exposed prominent collarbones and a flat sweep of bony chest before Tanner's undershirt covered her slight, thin tits. It couldn't hide her hard, thick nipples, though, and the sight deflected SueLynn from her original purpose.

She pulled Tanner to her feet with a quick jerk and stripped both shirts off her in one fast sweep. Tanner's britches bunched under the hemp rope that held them up and the facts of her life clicked into focus. "You been hungry some?"

Tanner shrugged. "More than most, I reckon, less than some." Her heavy hill accent had already hinted at her background, but her body showed harsh treatment. It wasn't right that some starved while others threw away buckets of food every night.

Tanner shivered in the sunset glow, a chill falling with the night. SueLynn gathered her close, pushing her furnace of a belly against the kid's ribcage. Working and eating like a man had fleshed her out, made her look like her papa and her uncles more than her willowy mama. Tanner wrapped her arms hard around SueLynn's back and squeezed with surprising strength.

Tanner had probably washed in the last stream just like SueLynn had, but that was a long day's march in the past. They each brought hard work and hot woman smell to a mix that blended as sweetly as she hoped their bodies would.

The skin of her belly tugged on Tanner's. Her nipple poked into Tanner's collarbone. No wonder SueLynn kept thinking of her as a kid. She was no bigger than a minute and so slight that her clothes were most likely swiped from a twelve-year-old brother.

The close-up feeling of Tanner's little body brought a stronger yearning to press her into the ground, to cover her and take her inside. SueLynn tugged the rigging knot free—this was a working woman who knew how a miner tied a load—and plunged her hand into the loose waistband of Tanner's britches.

Her private hair was thick and springy and everything down there was ten degrees hotter than the rest of Tanner's body. SueLynn wrapped her free arm around Tanner's waist, turning her just enough to keep digging, pushing, pulling, until the touch of wetness gave her the path to Tanner's inside parts. SueLynn bit Tanner's shoulder while her fingers found the way in between the long lips, untangling the hair protecting them. Tanner felt like a wet wedding dress and her hips bucked when SueLynn found the end of bone and the beginning of the birth canal, so soft and stretchy.

Fingers drenched, SueLynn pulled her hand up between those lips until she found the bit that moved back and forth when she rocked it between her fingers. Tanner drooped in her arms and spread her legs as much as she could. Her britches fell and caught on her straining thighs. SueLynn put a knee behind Tanner's and collapsed with her to the ground.

SueLynn landed on her knees and Tanner ended up straddling her thigh, back to front, legs trapped by her britches.

"I gotta get those off you." SueLynn dove forward, forcing Tanner down in front of her. Tanner's little round ass shone pale over the waist of the pants and SueLynn groaned with the throbbing of her private parts and the sense of sheer power she had over the smaller woman. She stripped the pants right off her and grabbed her up by the waist.

Tanner braced herself on her hands and knees and SueLynn pulled her ass close. Her own britches detracted from the feeling and she shucked them down to her knees without releasing Tanner. Wiry muscles bunched in Tanner's back when she thrust back. SueLynn lay on that strong back for support while one hand dove back in for Tanner's hot center and the other wrapped around to pull on her nipples.

Stroking in small, slow circles, SueLynn went back over and over for the angle that made Tanner arch her back and cry out. "More," she begged, and SueLynn pulled Tanner's legs apart to put one of her own between them. Tanner ground down on her thigh and whimpered when SueLynn went back to rubbing her. SueLynn pulled her upright so that Tanner balanced on her knees, rubbing her whole area on SueLynn. She held her fingers still and Tanner writhed in her confining arms. SueLynn bit Tanner's neck and watched herself pull at the big nipples on Tanner's little tits.

Tanner's smell got stronger and stronger and she started jerking in the middle of her rubbing. SueLynn took up the slack, moving her fingers just a little in the way Tanner had been using them to rub on. Tanner's motion changed to a fast thrust, dragging up and down SueLynn's thigh. SueLynn wrapped her arm tight around her ribs to keep her in place and bit her shoulder, hard.

Tanner's whole body tightened and released, over and over, until SueLynn wondered if she'd ever stop. When Tanner put both her hands on SueLynn's, she thought it was the signal to stop, but Tanner pushed her hand deeper, then whimpered.

The need in the sound spurred SueLynn. She pushed Tanner back onto her hands and raised her hips far enough to thrust two fingers into her fattened canal. Spare as Tanner was, this part of her was lush. SueLynn pushed Tanner's shoulders down to the ground, angling her ass even higher, and used her hip to lend force to her thrusts. Tanner's whimpers dropped to groans and her ass shook with the power of SueLynn's strong, miner's thighs and hips shoving her fingers deep and hard into Tanner's heat.

The backs of Tanner's thighs prickled the fronts of SueLynn's and the thin skin between her shoulder blades bunched with her attempts to brace herself. SueLynn's focus, strong as it was, didn't drown out her own aching need to be touched. She shuddered and wondered if she could get so excited she'd tumble over from Tanner's texture, her smell, her thrusting need.

Tanner's first quakes had felt never-ending, but her jolting cries rose and rose in pitch, circling higher like a hunting hawk until they spiraled into inhuman screams.

Tanner's hand disappeared between her legs and the sound cut off mid-breath, turned into huffs that mirrored the squeeze of Tanner's canal on SueLynn's fingers. That whole area tightened and released against SueLynn's hip, an entire sapling's-worth of resilience and strength in one secret womanly place.

When Tanner pulled off her fingers and collapsed, SueLynn shoved her forgotten britches off her feet and climbed Tanner's body again. She lay on her, arms along Tanner's arms, tits pressing into her shoulder blades, and soaked up the scent of her hair and the feel of her skin. Before long, though, she couldn't keep her hips from moving, circling above Tanner, wanting more.

Tanner pulled SueLynn's hand in close to her face, sniffed

and licked the fingers that had been inside her. SueLynn's scandalized shock was oil on fire. She rose onto all fours. "Roll over," she said to Tanner.

Tanner's squirming roll rubbed bits of her all over bits of SueLynn. When she reached her back, Tanner reached right up and twisted SueLynn's nipples. The confusing mix of pleasure and pain sent shudders through SueLynn that were equal parts pulling away and pushing closer. Tanner's skin on her inner thighs, her concave belly the perfect home for SueLynn's ponderous belly, these sensations only got stronger when Tanner pulled SueLynn's head down for another kiss.

Tanner nibbled lightly, tongued just inside SueLynn's lips. She pulled at SueLynn's upper lip with her teeth while licking it aggressively.

Tanner grinned, eyelids heavy. "I think I'm too limp to lay you down. Why don't you bring yourself up here. Put yourself where I can reach you with my mouth."

SueLynn groaned. "I want to, so bad. You got to tell me if I make it hard for you to breathe."

"If I pinch your foot, I need air. Otherwise, don't worry about me. I want you in my mouth."

SueLynn quivered, the words of desire pushing her hard, beyond whatever she'd known in the past. This was no furtive game between girls. Nothing to do in the dark and pretend never happened in the light of day.

The sky was dark blue, the color confusingly called midnight. A big moon lit the clearing well enough to see Tanner's body agleam, and her eyes seemed to glow with a light of their own. She could end up following that light to the ends of the earth.

SueLynn slid up and sat on Tanner's chest, staring at the narrow chin and the open mouth so close to parts of herself she knew only by feel. Tanner's hands gripped SueLynn's hips and tried to pull her forward.

"I want to look at you a minute," she said, her voice low. Tanner's hopelessness had infected her that much. SueLynn was no longer certain she would live through the battle to come. If she might could die tomorrow, she'd do everything she'd ever dreamt of doing first.

Tanner licked her lips, eyes on SueLynn's hair. "I can't wait to taste you. I touch myself and lick it off my fingers when I'm alone at home. You smell different, sharper. Your hair is shorter and I can see what's inside. I'm all closed up unless I spread myself out, but you're already pushing out to meet me."

SueLynn felt heavier and thicker with every word from Tanner's mouth. Her lips caressed the words and her tongue flashed out to form the Ls in alone and close. SueLynn reached down and pulled herself open a little farther.

"Oh, sweet Jesus, I can see your excitement. You shine in the moonlight like a photograph no one has painted color on. Come here, SueLynn. Come here and let me paint you."

Hearing her own name from those lips put a hook in her and Tanner reeled her in with a look. SueLynn rose, still holding back her lips, and settled down over Tanner's mouth.

Tanner's tongue flashed out to find her opening and slid up as far as it would go. SueLynn shifted down, cautiously, until she was inside Tanner's mouth. Tanner's lips did something and her tongue swirled slower than ice freezing. When it felt like too much, SueLynn slid forward. Tanner took the change in stride, tonguing her hole and all around, getting to every tiny piece of sensitive flesh. SueLynn pulled back down to offer her most sensitive bit and Tanner attacked. Teeth and lips and a strong, pulsing tongue.

SueLynn screeched, but she didn't pull back. She ground into the pain and pleasure, into the too-much of it all. Tanner's hand circled around from her hip to the back and dipped between her ass cheeks. She pushed her thumb into SueLynn at the same time she sucked hard and SueLynn bounced. Moving herself in Tanner's mouth felt so good that she moved again and leaned forward so Tanner could keep her thumb inside her. Tanner's knuckles rubbed all around her opening and SueLynn built a rhythm that used Tanner's mouth and hand to chase pleasure into a timeless place where there was nowhere better to be, nothing better to be doing.

Tanner knew better, it seemed. She sped her motions, and SueLynn realized that there was another place, another sensation she hadn't gotten to yet. Her tits bounced between her outstretched arms and her belly pressed the top of

Tanner's head. She had no idea how Tanner was breathing, but she trusted that Tanner would signal her if needs be.

The steady increase of delicious tension gained a hard edge and SueLynn froze. Tanner tried to move her head but was trapped, so she just used her lips and tongue and teeth. She bit at SueLynn.

SueLynn grunted and groaned, shaking over top of Tanner, thighs and belly and arms quaking. Tanner's thumb filled her, pushed back against the rock of her hips. She hadn't even realized she'd started moving again, but Tanner's teeth ground her soft flesh and her tongue rubbed hard.

SueLynn spasmed upright as though shot. Her arms jerked and her belly hardened and softened as though going through labor pains at great speed. When the tension poured out of her, she swayed and nearly fell, only to start laughing and lurch to the side. She rolled onto her back and reached for Tanner, eyes closed.

Tanner draped herself along SueLynn's side, leaning on her elbow to look down at her.

SueLynn opened her eyes to avoid getting lost in the feeling of Tanner's skin on hers. She didn't know if she would fall asleep or pull Tanner onto her if she did get lost, but she could hardly move for the moment. "You feel so good to me."

"You make me feel so good." Tanner sounded lighter than before, nearly like a different person. "Listen to us. What a pair."

"Can't say as I mind sounding silly after feeling like that. Were you hoping to get some sleep tonight?"

"No, sugar. We got better things to do than sleep."

THE GIRL AT THE WINDOW

BY CARA PATTERSON

1942: WWII: Russia

The smoke was thick and acrid.

Masha pulled her scarf up over her nose and mouth, narrowing her eyes until she could barely see the outline of the girl in front of her. She held onto the belt of Olga's coat, and felt Ludmilla do the same to her belt.

Getting separated was not an option, not with the crack of gunfire ahead and the bombers still growling through the smoke-obscured sky.

The ground was unstable beneath their feet, the rubble of shattered buildings obscuring the cobbles. Somewhere, someone was screaming, a shrill, insistent sob. Masha tried to stop her ears. She could not help them. There was a narrow window before the smoke cleared, and they had to get to their target.

Olga slowed and stopped. Masha did the same. A figure was ahead of them, a shadow approaching. Masha heard the click of Olga's pistol being cocked.

"This way!" It was barely a breath.

Masha's heart skipped a beat. Sergei Dorokhov. The scout assigned to guide them to their new base.

Olga relaxed, lowered her gun. She started moving again. Masha fell into step behind her. The rubble shifted strangely beneath her feet and she made the mistake of looking down. A soft arm jutted out beneath a broken wall, fingers crooked towards the sky. It was too pale to be living, the rubble around it stained red.

Masha swallowed hard, stepping over the limb. She heard Ludmilla gag behind her.

Dorokhov led them onwards. She didn't know how he could see through the smoke. Even the buildings closest to them were hazy shapes, but he darted on, swift as a hare, waiting for them to catch up. He led them into an alleyway, motioning them toward a small, narrow door.

"Along the corridor until you reach the hall. Climb until the fourth level," he whispered to each of them as they ducked beneath the lintel. "Wait for me there."

Weighed down by their rifles and packs, the climb was exhausting. The building was big, the staircases wrapping around the walls of a grand hallway. Each level opened onto a landing, and each landing led to another flight. From below, it looked too big. From above, it felt even more so.

Some of their own men stood in doorways, bloody, smoke-stained, and watched them pass in silence. Their rifles were to be respected. No man was willing to make an enemy of them today.

On the final landing they stumbled to a halt, panting. Masha braced one hand against the wall, and pulled the scarf from her face with the other.

"It has a roof, at least," she said hoarsely.

"Part of one," Ludmilla said, peering up. She glanced at Olga, who was leaning over the banister, watching the soldiers below. "Heh. Kazakova is already looking for her next conquest."

Olga glared at her. "You would think that, Luda," she said sourly. "I was looking for Dorokhov."

A grin crossed Luda's round face. "Well, he's not what you would call handsome..."

Masha left them arguing. They often did, but there was no ill-intent behind it. On the battlefield, there was little enough amusement to be had. Luda took pleasure teasing Olga, and Olga enjoyed biting back. Masha preferred the quiet.

She moved to a doorway, peering into one of the rooms. Parts of the floor were damaged, but the walls were still standing. Glass crunched beneath her boots as she stepped carefully across the threshold. Keeping to the wall, she edged around the side of the room until she could risk a glance from the empty window frame.

The smoke was clearing, and below, she could see a small square. Where there must have been grass once, there were now craters, the soil turned and blackened by bombs. An iron bench was twisted into a gnarled flower.

She pressed her shoulders to the window frame, darting a look at the buildings that flanked the square. On one side, there were only ruins. Even the Germans wouldn't be able to use those. To the right, the front of the building was shattered, but she could see the glint of metal that spoke of weapons within it.

Opposite, the building had lost much of its roof, but most of the façade was intact. Even a few of the windows were still whole.

Something moved in one of them. Masha pulled back, heart pounding. It would not look well on her record if she were killed with her gun at her back. She swung it down, her hands moving automatically in a series of motions that she could do in her sleep.

She risked a second glance, then another.

All the windows were empty, except one.

A girl was standing behind the pane of glass, looking out. With the frame around her, it almost looked like a painting, too serene to be any part of the surrounding destruction. She was twining her golden hair into a braid over her shoulder, but her fingers went still when she saw Masha. Her eyes widened in some emotion Masha couldn't identify. Shock? Fear?

"Petrovna!" Masha recoiled from the window, turning back to the door.

"Yes, Dorokhov?"

The scout raised a scarred eyebrow. "If you're finished making yourself a target," he said, "you have been assigned the next room over. Better sightlines on the square."

She rolled her eyes at him, but still made a deliberate show of edging back to the door and guarding her perimeter. She saw the amusement in his eyes. He was an older man, hands too knotted with age to wield a gun, but she had heard stories about his skill with a knife.

"There's a building across the square," she said, as he led her down the hall. "A girl was in the window."

Dorokhov spat in contempt. "Ah, yes," he said. "The little golden bird. She makes herself pretty for the soldiers. Puts her hair in braids, smiles for them."

"For the Germans?" Masha said, sickened.

Dorokhov's bowed shoulders rose in a shrug. "Their men have food," he said. "She paints herself like a whore and gets what she wants." He glanced back at Masha, then at her rifle. "You could show her a kindness. Put her out of her misery."

Masha's lips pressed together in a tight line. "My bullets are for Germans," she said. "I won't use them to spill Russian blood."

Dorokhov snorted. "She may have been born Russian, but her cunt is German now."

Masha glanced back at the doorway. "All the same," she said, "I won't kill one of our own people."

The old man shook his head. "What it is to be young," he muttered.

He pushed open a cracked door, revealing the main room of a large apartment. The furniture was in pieces, a torn couch pushed back against the wall. Piles of sandbags had been laid below the wide, empty window frame in readiness for her. A door opened off each side of the room, and she could see her comrades moving and arranging their kit.

"Kazakhova and Nesterova have one side each," Dorokhov said. He jerked his thumb at the left doorway. "There is another room at the back of that one which has no windows. You'll rest and eat there. You are all to remain on this level. The boys downstairs will remain there."

"Who is our commanding officer here?" she asked.

"Captain Ivanov, who will meet you soon," the man said.

She smiled briefly. "Thank you, Dorokhov."

He nodded and was gone.

Luda poked her head through the doorway. "Not bad," she said. "More walls than I expected. And a room with a roof to sleep in. I think we got lucky."

Masha knelt down by the couch to unpack her kit in silence. Being in Stalingrad was not what anyone could call lucky.

The building wasn't a bad place to be located. They had been brought in because the Germans were trying to push back and claim the streets to bring them closer to the river. They needed to maintain the supply lines, but Masha was proud to be a part of the army holding them back.

The square marked the boundary of the German territory, and where the Russians held the line. Trenches carved through the road, some begun by falling bombs, others dug in the night by men who tried to use the mask of cloud to hide their activities.

Masha took one of them one night.

The metal of her gun was cool against her cheek as she watched them. They kept low. They knew they were being observed. She had learned patience long ago, when her father taught her how to take a life. It wasn't the same, but if she thought of it that way, it was easier. She lay still. She watched. She breathed soft and slow.

The crack of her shot split the air. Her target folded, the spray of blood and bone staining the rubble behind him. The Germans scattered like frightened deer. Masha reloaded her rifle, taking her time. They would be wary now, their heads down. There would be no more targets for her tonight.

She always liked the night watch best of all.

When the bombers weren't flying, and it was quiet, it was almost beautiful. On nights of a full moon, when it was too bright to venture into the streets, and no one set foot out of doors, the world was painted silver. The cloudy nights were the ones to be wary of. That was when their enemies would try and steal the advantage, and that was when she was always on her guard.

She glanced out across the square, brought up short by a pale figure in the window.

The little golden bird, Dorokhov called her. She was in the same window, her hair loose around her shoulders, her hand pressed against the glass.

She was looking down at the body of the fallen man. From the position of her building, she would have a clear view of his face. She stared at him, then looked across the square to the darkened window where Masha was hidden in shadows.

Perhaps he was one of her men, Masha thought with a grimace of distaste. Maybe she mourned one of her customers.

The girl was still staring at the window. Masha raised her face enough to be seen, and then, to her surprise, the girl smiled. The expression illuminated her pale, thin face, and just as suddenly as the smile had come, it—and she—vanished back into the darkness of the room behind her.

Masha frowned, staring across at the window.

She said nothing of it to Olga or Luda. They shared Dorokhov's view that anyone who colluded with their enemy was as bad as the enemy themselves. Olga muttered viciously that one day, she would put a bullet through that skinny white neck. Who knew what secrets the girl was telling, she said angrily. Who knew how far her betrayals extended?

For all that they called her a whore, no one came or went from her building for days. When she did emerge one evening, it was as Dorokhov described: her hair was beautifully braided, her dress was neat. She sat on the steps of the building, as if she was just taking air.

"Looking for her friends," Luda said darkly, turning away from her rifle.

Masha said nothing, fixing her sights on the girl. She was older than Masha had realised, perhaps closer to twenty than fifteen, but she was small and thin, which made her look more fragile. She turned suddenly, looking into one of the alleys that framed the building. Masha barely had time to sight the man or his uniform before the girl was leading him up the steps.

The door closed, and Masha felt bile rise in her throat. She pressed her mouth to her sleeve, and drew breaths through it to keep from being sick. The very idea of being touched by someone like that made her skin crawl.

How desperate, she wondered, did a girl have to be, to succumb to the touches of a man like that?

She only chanced to glance back at the building a moment

later, and saw the movement in the usual window. She knew she shouldn't look. It felt shameful, her face growing hot, but she found she couldn't look away.

By the evening light, she could make out a little of the room: pale walls, what might be a bed, and curtains. A normal room for a good little Russian girl to whore herself out. Something wasn't right, though. She tilted the rifle and the scope to see better.

The girl was alone. She was leaning against the door of the room, and her pretty dress was no longer so pretty. The front was dark, wet, clinging to her. She lifted her right hand, brushing hair back from her cheek with her knuckles, and Masha saw the knife.

She crossed to the window, and looked towards Masha's window. She couldn't see Masha, of that Masha was sure, but she still smiled, fresh blood smudged on her pale cheek, before she shut the curtain and closed the world out.

Masha didn't know what to make of it.

The soldier certainly hadn't emerged from the building, but was she to believe that the slip of a girl had killed him? It didn't seem possible. She didn't say anything to the others, keeping the golden-haired girl's secrets.

It wouldn't help if they knew she liked the nights of the full moon better now, because the girl would push up her window and sit in the moonlight, her gold turned silver, smiling at the sky. Masha's comrades at arms always believed she was dreaming of a sweetheart back home. She let them believe it. It was safer, and looking at a beautiful golden girl hurt no one.

It was several days before Masha realised that the girl knew she was being watched, when the girl gave her an unexpected gift.

It was a late afternoon watch. The sun was high but the chill in the air misted her breath. The girl emerged from her building, her eyes down as she made her way to the water pump on the far side of the square. There was no combat expected, so all eyes were on her. Masha watched her through the scope of her rifle. She was carrying two buckets, though it was clear she was too slight to manage both.

All the same, she filled both buckets and was struggling

along on the edge of the trench with them. A German in the trench reached up, steadying one bucket. He kept his head down, but the girl didn't bend to take the bucket back. She fumbled with the other, then reached out. He had to rise up, and she smiled, hauling the bucket up. It could have been the shift in weight which made her totter sideways. It could have been a fortunate coincidence.

Instinct moved Masha's fingers.

The German was flung back by the impact of the bullet through his eye. The girl screamed, dropping to the ground and covering her head with her arms. The buckets of water spilled. Gunfire broke out above her, and the girl crawled desperately back towards her building. Half-concealed by a balustrade, she sagged there, as if too terrified to move.

It was only when Masha tilted her scope toward the girl that she saw the quiet smile on her face. Pale fingertips touched the girl's lips, then she scrambled up and ran through the doors of the building, slamming them behind her.

Masha stared at the doors blankly. The Germans had been hiding for days, but one misstep by a golden-haired girl had given her the perfect shot.

It couldn't have been a coincidence.

Still, she said nothing to her comrades.

Days drifted by. Sometimes, not a single shot was fired. On other days, the square was almost overrun as their forces tried to hold the Germans at bay.

Masha once believed she would never be able to sleep on a battlefield, but after a dozen hours of ceaseless fighting, she sometimes fell asleep with her cheek still pressed to her rifle. Even the cold wasn't enough to stop her drifting, when the exhaustion got too much.

Their defence was having an impact.

The square was no longer the boundary of the German territory. Their soldiers had been pushing back, supported by the snipers. More houses had been reclaimed. The ground, crisp with snow, was littered with bodies. They were half-hidden in the drifts now, friend indistinguishable from enemy.

For a brief moment, there was a respite. Scouts were looking for safe routes to move the snipers forward. Masha bit down on her tongue, and tried not to think about leaving the building. She polished her kit, watched, and listened as Olga and Luda bickered. With no targets left, they huddled together in the windowless room.

They were in there when the cry went up from the lower levels. Bombers were in the air.

Masha scrambled up, rushing to her window to look out. The sky was clear. She could see the planes coming in. The Germans didn't want to cede their territory. Without their men there, they had no reason to hold back.

She spun around. "Luda! Olga!" she screamed, snatching up her gun and rushing for the door.

The first bomb hit the far side of the square, the vibrations from the impact making her teeth rattle. They were rats in a trap, they knew, but better to be closer to the ground, to get out, rather than fall with the building. They raced for the stairs, the men below already on their way down.

High above, the roof took a direct hit. Masha slammed herself back against the wall, as masonry and tile cascaded in. Luda wasn't fast enough. She grabbed at thin air as the landing beneath her gave way. Olga screamed, reaching out.

They could only watch her fall.

The building was burning, and more of the roof was falling in. Masha grabbed Olga's arm, dragging her—weeping—on. Tears could be shed later. The stairs were intact for now, and they ran. Another bomb hit somewhere close by, shaking the building again. It was coming down in pieces now. A spar of wood struck her as it fell, but she barely felt it, spurred on by terror.

The men of their unit had scattered around the square. Masha reeled around. Her head hurt, and there was blood running hotly down her neck.

"Here!" A voice. Female. Young. Masha squinted around and saw the door of the building across the square. It was open, and a familiar face was there. The girl was beckoning urgently. "There's room in here!"

Between the falling bombs and the craters and the screaming and dying, it felt like a trek through hell. The other survivors had poured into the building already, but the girl only stepped forward to catch Masha's arm.

On Masha's other side, Olga pulled her away from the girl. "Don't you touch Petrovna," she snarled.

The little bird's expression went waxen, and she released Masha's arm. "She's hurt."

A plane roared overhead.

"We don't have time to fight," Masha murmured, swaying. She leaned forward, and caught the girl's arm. She was soft, and somehow, warm. "Inside. Now."

The girl motioned them in, pushing the doors shut behind them. The building looked so similar to the one they had left behind that Masha stopped short. Her head felt light.

"What's that stink?" Captain Ivanov snapped, pushing through the cluster of soldiers gathered in the hall.

The little bird had her eyes on the floor. "I wasn't strong enough to take the garbage out," she said meekly, pointing to a doorway. Ivanov didn't take her eyes off her, but jerked his head. One of the soldiers darted through, down a small staircase, then recoiled.

"Dead men, Captain!" he exclaimed. "At least five. Maybe more. All with their throats cut."

The little bird raised her face. Masha saw the defiance in her eyes.

Ivanov stared at her. "We're taking this building," he said. "Is it sound?"

"First and second levels on the left side are," the girl replied. "Beyond that, the stairs are broken and the floors are damaged. Only light people can go up higher. The roof caved in at the back." She jerked her head towards Masha and Olga. "They get the upper rooms."

Masha, swaying, didn't hear any more. Her vision was clouding, and she heard someone cry out her name as she fell. When her senses returned, she was lying on a soft surface. She opened her eyes, peering about. A bed, with pale linens and a knitted blanket. The walls around her were pale, and through the half-open window, she could see a building burning.

Her building.

"Your friend didn't want to stay."

Masha pushed herself up on one arm, searching for the

speaker. She didn't have to look far. The girl was rinsing blood out of a cloth in a wash bowl on a dusty table.

The girl looked at her. "You won't want to go," she said knowingly. She returned to the bed and sat down. The cloth was cool and damp when she brushed it to Masha's aching temple. "I know you want to stay here."

Masha sank back against the pillow. "You know that?"

"Mm." The girl brushed strands of Masha's dark hair back from her brow. "I know you were watching me."

Masha forced herself to recall her training, how to stay still and quiet, when everything in her wanted to scramble up, run, hide. Staring at the girl had seemed harmless when there was no chance they would meet. Now? Now, her comrades would hate her as much as they hated the girl in front of her, if they knew why she stared.

"They said you colluded with the enemy," she said quietly.

"They did," the girl said. "Many do." She rose and went to rinse the cloth again. "My family died in the first raids. I survived by luck." She twisted the cloth. "Sometimes, luck runs out." She smiled at the bloody water. "My father taught me how to defend myself, so I did." Grey eyes returned to Masha. "I have remained lucky."

Masha had to look away from her, and closed her eyes. "You spoke with Germans." It was a fact to hold onto, that she had demeaned herself, interacted with the enemy, an act of treason.

"Yes," the girl said. "Before I slid my knife into them." The bed shifted as she sat back down. "You are saying all the things they say. What do you say, Marya Petrovna? Do you tell me you looked for so many nights because you wanted to see the face of your enemy?" There was a gently-mocking note in her voice. "Were you memorising your target?"

Masha opened her eyes. The girl was watching her, eyebrows raised.

"What else was I meant to look at?" Her voice was not as sharp as she wanted it to be.

Grey eyes lit up when the girl smiled. "Anything," she said. She swiped the last of the blood from Masha's brow. "Now, you are to rest."

Masha watched her dart to the window, pulling the curtains closed to hide the ruins. She was no longer in her pretty dresses. She had trousers – too big for her – beneath layers of dresses and a jacket on top. She even wrapped a scarf around her head.

"To keep them from looking," she said, noticing Masha's eyes on her. "I may be an enemy in their eyes, but there are few women here they can use."

Masha knew that was true. She, Olga, and Luda were spared their attentions because they were useful. Still, if the men took it into their heads to have the girl, no amount of clothing would stop them. "Be careful," she said.

The girl's thin features softened in a smile. "I have luck," she said, patting a knife tucked in her belt.

She was almost at the door, when Masha realised something.

"Wait!" she said, raising herself from the pillow. "Your name. You never told me."

Grey eyes shone. "Svetlana Volkova," the girl replied, then she was gone.

Bright wolf, Masha thought. It was fitting. Not a bird. A wolf with teeth.

Outside, in the wake of the bombings, the Germans were trying to push the bloodied remains of the Russian forces back. Every gun shot, every scream, every grenade, made Masha's head throb unbearably. She wanted to be by the window, armed, but it would be a waste of bullets to try and shoot when she could barely move.

She slept. Perhaps it was only unconsciousness. She couldn't be sure with the world growing hazy at the edges. Once, Olga was there, searching her pockets for spare ammunition. Once, Ivanov tried and rouse her, then shook his head and said something unintelligible to someone behind him.

Masha hated feeling useless, but by the time she could lift her head again, all was quiet in the streets. She pushed herself from the bed, stumbling to the window. The drapes were thick, and her hands felt clumsy as she opened them.

The building that had been their base was nothing more than smoking rubble. She stared at it, wondering how many others died with Luda as it came down.

"They've retreated."

Masha didn't turn, still watching the dull glow of the smouldering ruins. "Which side?"

Volkova laughed. "Them," she said. "The ones we kill."

She closed the door with a kick, and Masha looked around. Volkova was carrying a bowl in one hand, and a flask in the other. Masha could smell the food, and her stomach ached. It had been so long since she had eaten.

"Where did you get that?" she asked, watching the girl warily as Volkova sat down on the edge of the bed.

Volkova smiled, her teeth white. "Do you really want to know? Or would you prefer to eat?" She set down the flask and patted the bed beside her.

Hunger outweighed wariness. The bowl of slop was warm, thickened with grain.

"They tried to pay me," Volkova said, as Masha gulped down the food. "The ones I left to rot. Poor little Russkie. Doesn't speak German. Give her food, and she'll lift her skirt for you." She offered Masha the flask of water. "Wash it down. It makes the taste bearable."

Masha swallowed the water, so cold it stung her lips. "Why are you being kind to me?" she asked, too tired to be anything but blunt.

Volkova gazed at her. "Because you watched me," she said. She lifted her hand, gently smoothing Masha's hair back from her cheek.

"Many did," Masha whispered.

Volkova shook her head. "They hated—hate me," she said. "I saw you, Marya Petrovna, on the nights when the moon was full. You watched me, as I watched you."

Her fingertips were callused, rough on Masha's cheek. Her eyes searched Masha's face, and Masha thought her chest might burst if she could not remember how to breathe.

"You watched me?" Masha could barely believe it. "Why?"

Volkova's palm was warmer than her fingertips, and she answered by bringing their cold, chapped lips together. Warmth rushed through Masha's body, making her heart race, and the bowl slipped from her hands, falling to the floor. She caught Volkova's arm, but whether to push her back or pull her closer, she could not decide.

They jerked apart at the sound of boots on the landing, and Volkova rose, snatching up the bowl from the floor.

"Rest, Masha," she said, her pale cheeks flushed with colour. "Your Captain will need you soon."

Masha was left in the empty bedroom, the taste of barley and Volkova on her lips.

It was only the first kiss they shared.

With the men restricted to the lower levels, and Olga unwilling to share the air with someone she considered a traitor, they were left alone much of the time.

Volkova dragged in sandbags, and they set up a rifle bay at the window. They lay together there, and Masha felt her cheeks redden as she showed the girl how to fire her rifle. Volkova's body curved against hers, her back to Masha's chest, and they breathed together.

When the rifle kicked, Volkova laughed in sharp delight and turned to look at her. They found one another's lips again. It was better the second time, without the shock of the first. Volkova was bold. Her tongue flickered against Masha's lips, and Masha felt herself blushing again.

Volkova just grinned like a wolf, and turned back to the rifle.

When the streets were quiet, and night fell, Volkova would crawl into her bed, draw back the blankets in wordless offer. At first, Masha—flustered—slept beneath her coat by her gun, though the windows were cracked and the bitter chill was making her hands ache.

With each kiss, the lure of the bed grew. If they could be so warm from a handful of stolen kisses, how much warmer would it be to wrap around one another?

The fact that she thought of Volkova's hands on her had nothing to do with it when she laid down her gun and crept over to the bed. Volkova's braid curled across her throat, her arm tucked beneath her head. Masha hesitated, and would have turned back if Volkova's lips had not curved into a sweet smile. Without opening her eyes, she pushed back the blanket.

"No boots," she murmured.

Masha sat down on the edge of the bed, unlacing them. She felt the bed shift, felt Volkova move closer, felt a hand brush her side. "I have never done this before," she confided.

Volkova laughed. "Neither have I," she confessed, "but I know I want to touch you."

Masha left the boots on the floor and pulled her legs up onto the bed. There was little light coming between the curtains, but enough to see Volkova's eager face.

For the first time, Masha was the one to kiss her. If Volkova could be so bold, then she could too. It earned a soft moan from the other woman, as Volkova dragged the blankets back around them both. Nimble fingers loosened the buttons of Masha's coat and shirt, as Masha loosened the silky cascade of Volkova's hair.

Volkova's hands were as warm as Masha's were cold. Volkova's squeal was stifled urgently by a clumsy kiss as Masha covered one small breast. The squeal turned into a short, breathless gasp when Masha teased her nipple. She had no idea if others were sensitive as she was. Volkova, it seemed, was. The fierce, proud expression had given was to wide-eyed lust, her eyes jet-dark.

"Good?" Masha hazarded, smiling truly.

Volkova's hand was beneath her shirt, matching her touch. Masha arched her back encouragingly, and she keened softly in protest when the hand moved. Volkova's eyes held Masha's as she slid her hand slowly downwards, pushing beneath the loose belt of Masha's trousers. Masha's breathing caught, her tongue pressing to her lower lip.

"Open for me?" Volkova's voice was almost a plea, and Masha realised her legs were closed tight against Volkova's questing fingers. She shifted, rolling to her back and splayed her knees. Volkova leaned over her to kiss her again, grateful, greedy. Her golden hair fell about their faces as her fingers stroked through the dark curls between Masha's legs. Her touch was light and Masha's lips trembled against Volkova's.

It was one thing to imagine, but another entirely to feel callused fingertips that were not her own touching her so intimately. She knew she was warm and wet there already, as eager as Volkova, and yet, Volkova was getting none.

Masha pulled back from her kisses, her eyes on Volkova's face. She hissed softly between her teeth as two fingers rubbed against her in slow circles, which expanded and shrank with each circuit, making her hips lift in demand.

Her breath was coming quickly, and she lifted one hand to pluck open the front of Volkova's dresses, one by one. With each button, Volkova's fingertips rewarded her with a change in pressure. When she bared Volkova's breasts to the thin light, she had to bite down on her lip as a single slender finger slowly slid within her, and Volkova's thumb stroked her again.

"You want to look?" Volkova's voice was hoarse.

Masha had no words left. They were not her strength. Instead, she put her arm behind Volkova's back and tugged. She was so light that it was no effort to drag her up enough, pull her forward, and for Masha's mouth to find one of those rose-pink nipples.

Volkova's hand jerked against her, and Masha stifled a chuckling groan. A good response, then. Volkova's finger slipped free, but it returned a moment later, with another, and Volkova sank them deep, the heel of her hand pressing where her thumb had been before. The intensity of the pressure made Masha's mouth drop open, her breath catching, and she pulled Volkova closer again, suckling hard upon her breast, demanding more.

Her hand dragged around, pushing up under the skirts around Volkova's waist, tugging at the trousers that separated them. Volkova squirmed as much as she could, one hand braced on the pillow by Masha's head, the other stroking over, and deeper, and harder between her thighs.

When Masha's fingers found their way beneath the trousers, and stroked against Volkova, Volkova's whole body spasmed. She was whispering under her breath, meaningless nonsense, punctuated with Masha's name. Her hand was stuttering, but Masha could forgive her that for the way her face was flushed and her breath was hot and her hair loose. The cool, controlled girl was gone and Svetlana whimpered and squirmed against Masha's hand and lips.

Masha's other hand slipped down to join Svetlana's between her thighs, covering Svetlana's fingers with her own, pressing them deep, as she pushed her own fingers slowly into Svetlana's warmth. Against both of her hands, their hips rose and shifted, and her mouth went slack against Svetlana's breast. She was panting, and Svetlana was shuddering over her, and she could feel the tightness of Svetlana's body around her fingers, could feel the tremor in Svetlana's hand.

She threw back her head, gasping faintly, grinding against their joined hands, her eyes searching out Svetlana's face. Svetlana was staring wide-eyed at her, her cheeks wet. She was braced on her arm against the pillow, her hips jerking in tight, hard thrusts against Masha's hand. She caught her breath, her thighs trembling around Masha's hand, and gave a small, shrill cry.

She sank then, spent, and panting, and slowly, her hand started to move again, guided by Masha's own. Her thumb flickered, her fingers twisting, and she brought her mouth down on Masha's, her lips salty with tears. Masha stroked her thigh, smothering her own groan of release into Svetlana's flushed, pink mouth.

In the stillness, the only sound was their breathing.

Masha dragged one hand up, brushing against Svetlana's cheek, catching the last tears. "Bad?" she whispered.

Svetlana caught her hand, kissed her fingers. "Good," she replied in a whisper. "The first since my family..." She silenced herself against Masha's palm.

Masha curled her fingers against Svetlana's cheek. "The first of many good things to come," she offered quietly, hopefully. "This war won't last forever."

She could feel the heat of fresh tears against her palm. "Yes," Svetlana whispered, "when they're all dead."

Masha nodded. The last little wolf needed vengeance for her pack. "When we are done," she promised, and kissed her again. If they lived through the remains of the war, they had both earned the right.

MOMENT OF PEACE

BY JOVE BELLE

1945: WWII: South Pacific

Rose set the last of the dinner dishes in the industrial stainless steel sink as the opening strains of the show filtered through the canvas walls of the kitchen. The suds had long since given up and the water was tepid at best, and she wondered for the hundredth time why she thought joining the WACs was a good idea. She was doing the same exact thing she'd done all her life, cleaning up after messy men who never thought to say thank you. Only now, instead of her father and brothers, she did it for the hundreds of soldiers on an island she hadn't known existed until she received her orders. So much for weapons maintenance, the job Uncle Sam promised her. Sure, she'd been shown where that job was done just before they told her there was no need and sent her to the kitchen.

"Oh, Rose, it's starting. Hurry." Alma was a petite woman, slight in stature, and easily overlooked. But her mind was sharp. Sharp enough to get her assigned to communications, but not sharp enough to keep from being reassigned to the kitchen along with Rose. Still, Rose admired the way she paid attention and caught details others missed. Like how they were constantly coming up short on forks. Alma was the one who discovered that a few of the soldiers were trading them with the locals for handmade trinkets to send home. Rose hadn't even considered that. She was frustrated by the loss and annoyed that her ass kept getting chewed over it but never once did she think it was intentional. Who steals forks for God's sake?

"We're almost done." Rose rinsed a plate and handed it to Alma. "Only a few more left."

"I don't want to miss anything important." Alma's dishtowel was more wet than dry at this point, and all she managed to do was push the moisture around on the plate without actually drying anything. Rose didn't care. She'd signed up to serve her country during the war, but she hadn't thought that would literally mean serve them breakfast, lunch, and dinner.

"They'll start with the news reels." Rose finished the last plate and drained the water in the sink. She knew everything she needed to know. The Japanese bombed Pearl Harbor, the United States of America jumped into the Second World War, and Rose watched her brothers march away while their neighbors cheered. Two years later, after the speedy victory they'd been promised hadn't happened, the army changed their opinion about women serving during wartime. Nobody cheered when she signed up, but she figured that was fine. She still wanted to do her part, and the victory garden behind her house wasn't enough.

"Oh, I love the news." Alma sighed in a way that shouldn't have made Rose's stomach tighten, but it did. She gazed at Alma, finally done with the work and able to enjoy the reason she'd volunteered to stay late and let the others go back to the barracks early. Alma's eyes took on a faraway look as though she were remembering a more romantic place and time. That's what Alma did. She romanticized everything, saw things with little hearts drawn around the outside edges. Still, no matter how many times she saw Alma with that dreamy little smile, Rose's breath caught in her throat and she couldn't stop the grin from climbing up her face.

"Here." Rose reached for the last dish and the towel. Her fingers brushed against Alma's and the charged thrill made her pause in motion. She stopped, hand on the plate, barely touching Alma, and completely unable to remember how to breathe. They stared at each other for several long moments and the dreamy look in Alma's eyes was replaced by something darker, something needier. Instead of a tingle, this time Rose's stomach clenched.

Alma broke contact first. "Yes...um...right." She drew her hands away and held them behind her back. She looked anywhere but at Rose.

Rose finished with the plate, tossed the towel into the laundry bag, and picked up the stack of plates. It was just heavy enough to make her biceps flex and the small intake of breath told her that Alma noticed, too. Rose wore her uniform with the shirt sleeves rolled up. She'd started that as soon as she'd connected Alma's soft sighs to the movement of her arms. Rose tightened her grip to accentuate her muscles, and lifted the plates onto the shelf. When she finished, she dusted her hands together, then turned to Alma. "All done. You ready to go?"

Alma sucked in her bottom lip and held it between her teeth for a moment. It was such a subconsciously sexy thing that Rose gripped the edge of the sink to hold herself in place. If Alma knew she was doing it, she'd stop out of embarrassment and Rose didn't want that to happen. Their relationship was in a weird, strained place, stuck between friends and something more. They shared heated looks, and even a few kisses that could have been more, but Alma still went on dates with a skinny private who was so young he had acne and his face turned red when he tried to hold Alma's hand. Rose hated him on principle alone.

Rose smiled, lopsided and cocky because Alma liked it when she smiled like that. Alma still hadn't responded to Rose's question; she simply stood there, biting her lip as her eyes grew darker and her face flushed with heat. Rose took a small step toward her, just enough to let Alma see her interest, but not enough to push. "You wanna go clean up first? Or is Phillip waiting for you?"

Alma shook her head, a confused almost smile on her lips. "No date tonight. I..."

A thrill bloomed inside her and Rose took another careful step forward. "You...what?"

Alma took a deep breath, squared her shoulders, and looked Rose right in the eyes. "I want to spend the evening with you." Her bluster faded a bit and she hastily added, "If that's what you want, I mean."

Rose nodded, and even though she could feel her head bobbling like a doll at a carnival, she couldn't stop herself. "Yes, I definitely want."

"Good." Alma wrung her hands together, a nervous, pensive look on her face. She nodded once, then said more firmly, "Good."

Rose wanted to go to her right then, to take her into her arms and kiss her like she'd wanted for months. Not some abortive anxious kiss she feared would end as suddenly as it started, but a real, bodies pressed together, moan-wrenching, lips-parted kiss. But Alma looked just uncertain enough that Rose held herself back.

The crowd gathered for the show roared with applause and the sound pulled their attention away from each other. It gave Rose an opportunity to think without the heavy scrutiny of Alma's gaze upon her. She wanted to do this right. To make sure Alma never regretted her choice to tell Phillip no and Rose yes.

On the surface, that seemed like such a simple choice, one Rose had no trouble making. She chose Alma over everyone else. But she also knew it wasn't that easy for Alma. She was learning something new about herself. Rose had opened a door to possibilities that Alma hadn't even considered before. Not that she'd told Rose that, but Rose remembered that feeling, as if the earth had shifted beneath her and she'd realized that what she thought was the floor was actually the wall. Her first kiss with another woman had introduced her to the true laws of gravity and she'd landed on her ass with a thud. Eventually, though, she'd regained her footing and stood stronger than ever before.

Ever since their first heated glance, Rose had been watching for signs that Alma was finally back on her feet and standing on the correct surface. Tonight, Alma looked as if she might actually be there, but Rose couldn't be sure. There was still hesitation in Alma's voice and in the way her gaze darted periodically toward the main entrance. Rose had gotten over that twitchy, obsessive need to make sure no one else was around, but that was only after realizing that if she paid attention in the right ways, she could tell when others were around. For now, they were alone.

"Do you know who's on stage tonight?" Alma asked. There had to be more to the question because it felt out of place after her announcement that she wanted to spend the evening with Rose, not Phillip.

The USO tour provided a bright spot in an otherwise bleak situation. This island had once been beautiful, Rose could see the shadow of splendor all around, but it'd been overtaken by foot soldiers, gun fire, and landmines. "Some comedian. I'm not sure."

"Oh, do you still want to go?" This time Alma took a step toward Rose. Her movement was tentative and she faltered, but she never looked away.

This was all new. Normally, Rose was the one who circled, the one who advanced, the one who stole kisses and listened to the strangled moans that Alma tried to swallow down. God, she wanted everything Alma was intimating, but what if she was wrong? What if Alma wanted to sit in the bleachers and secretly hold hands rather than the very un-chaste vision Rose had for what came next?

"Whatever you want." Even if Rose was off base, she still needed to be closer to her than the few feet that still separated them. She decided that Alma would tell her to stop if she went too far, and quickly closed the gap between them before she lost her nerve.

Alma's eyes widened, but she didn't step back. She swallowed hard and nodded her head a little too enthusiastically. "Okay."

Rose let her hand settle lightly on Alma's hip. She didn't want to scare her away, but she also really wanted to be connected with her, however minimally. The heat of Alma's body soaked through the rough material of her uniform and warmed Rose more than one simple touch should have. She moved her thumb gently in a slow, steady arc, rising and falling along the curve of Alma's waist.

"I'm going to kiss you, okay?" Rose whispered, impressed that her voice didn't break. She'd never been so patient with a woman before. Then again, she'd never been so taken with one either. Rose had enjoyed more than her fair share of encounters, but rarely did the emotional connection come close to the physical reaction. They were, for the most part, need-based events. But Alma? This was all new for her. Rose could tell by the way she hesitated, by the way her gaze lingered when she thought no one was looking, and in the way her body trembled as she tried to decide if she should give in and say yes, or run away like the good girl she was raised to be. Rose was willing to wait as long as she needed to.

Alma sucked her bottom lip between her teeth again, a gesture Rose had learned meant that she was nervous and excited and unsure all at once. Rose closed her eyes for a moment to keep herself from claiming that worried bottom lip as her own. Without meaning to, she tightened her grip on Alma's waist. Alma gasped and Rose's eyes snapped open. That wasn't a gasp that said stop. It said please, more, and don't stop. Slowly, she raised her other hand to cup the side of Alma's face, her fingers tangling into Alma's hair, and her palm flush with her cheek.

"Please." Rose was close to begging and if she thought it would help, she would drop to her knees. Once there, though, she wouldn't want to get up until she tasted the heat between Alma's thighs, something she wasn't sure Alma was ready for. The image of Alma with her head thrown back as Rose coaxed her to orgasm with her tongue made her groan quietly.

Alma stared at Rose through her lashes, a cute, coquettish move that made Rose weak at the knees. Haltingly, Alma nodded, her movement jerky as if her mind and body couldn't quite agree on the answer. Then, the sweetest, softest "yes" passed through her lips and Rose brought herself close enough for Alma's hot, stuttered breath to puff against her skin. She tightened her grip in the tangle of curls that had started to escape their barrette. She tilted Alma's head back until their gazes met once again, and Alma's lips parted with a small, plaintive whimper.

Slowly, oh so slowly, Rose brushed her mouth over Alma's. It wasn't their first kiss, but it felt infinitely more important than the ones that came before, largely because of what Rose hoped would come next. It was also the first time she asked permission.

The first time had been a farce. Alma had teased her in just the right way and, before she could stop herself, Rose lunged into the space between them and took Alma's breath away with a heated, sharp kiss that ended far too quickly. Alma had blushed and Rose's lips tingled in a way that stopped her short. She'd always enjoyed a nice kiss, but never had the experience left her feeling electrocuted. She'd touched her lips in wonder and stepped away with a muttered, "Sorry."

The second time, neither of them were surprised. Alma had been on a date with Phillip and a fire of some unknown, unreasonable emotion had risen through Rose, growing hotter and hotter with every passing minute. Eventually, Alma returned to their shared tent, thankfully before their other two roommates. Rose had descended upon her, bracing her hand on the support pole to the side of Alma's head and leaning in close enough to make Alma's chest rise and fall like it did the first time they kissed.

"Did you have fun?" she'd asked, her voice heavy with...something. Alma had nodded, wide eyed. Her gaze slid from Rose's eyes to her lips and that's when Rose took her

She'd kissed her hard and greedily, pushing her tongue between Alma's lips and tasting the sweet fruit she'd eaten for dessert. They'd stayed like that, gasping and pleading and wrapped in the most heated kiss of Rose's life until they heard the sounds of their roommates returning for the night. She'd pulled away with a groan and turned as she wiped her hand over her mouth.

If she were a man, Rose wouldn't have stopped. She would have allowed herself to linger with her lips on Alma's, allowed them to be caught. If she were a man, she'd be clapped on the back and called a dog or a stud or whatever other stupid names the soldiers called each other when they discussed their conquests. But, she wasn't a man. She was a woman who desperately wanted to be with another woman, to touch her in all the right places. Those places, however, would be judged as very wrong if they were caught. Instead of congratulations, she'd be court marshaled and dishonorably discharged. And so would Alma. She cared too much to let that happen.

She hadn't look at Alma again until after she was in her hammock with her blanket snugged up around her face to hide the flush in her cheeks. Alma's lips were dark and swollen and the other roommates teased her about her hot date with a certain private. She'd simply nodded and glanced briefly at Rose before moving to her own bunk to sleep.

The last time they'd kissed, it took Rose by surprise. She wanted Alma, on that she was clear. She'd never been great at denying her desires or holding herself back once she'd identified something—or someone—she wanted. This was different. *Alma* was different. She was clearly surprised by her reaction to Rose. Surprised and uncertain. She continued to date Phillip, all the while shooting Rose these pleading, needy looks. And Rose *really* wanted to show Alma everything she was missing, everything Phillip could never give her. She held herself back, not because she thought Alma would reject her, but because of the slight taint of fear that mingled with the desire in Alma's eyes. Rose couldn't tell if it was fear of her, fear of how she felt, or fear of something much larger. Until Alma was ready, she refused to take what Alma offered. Alma deserved more than desperate rutting in the few stolen moments when no one else was around.

One night, she and Alma were alone in their tent, the other women at an impromptu dance in the dining hall. Alma didn't go and Rose didn't question it. They sat on opposite ends of Alma's cot and played cards. Between them, they drank a bootleg fifth of whiskey Rose's friend had sent to her, wrapped inside a pair of new wool socks. As if she needed her feet to be any hotter on this damned island. But the whiskey had been an excellent addition to the night. The more they drank, the darker Alma blushed and the more Rose laughed.

Rose didn't know how they went from laughing and drinking and slapping the jacks in the deck, to being wrapped inexplicably together. She must have kissed Alma and not the other way around because that's the only thing that made sense, even with the whiskey coursing through them. They kissed slowly, languidly, in a heated wave of lips and tongues. They kissed long enough for Rose to ease Alma onto her back as she consumed the whiskey on Alma's breath. They kissed long enough for her body to flood with desire and for Alma's arousal to overwhelm her. They kissed long enough for her leg to slip between Alma's thighs and for her to rock her hips, making them both groan. They kissed until Rose remembered that she'd promised herself she wouldn't take Alma this way.

Between the alcohol and her lust, it took everything in her to push herself away from Alma. Her arms shook and she couldn't think beyond the clouded haze of want. Alma had whimpered and grabbed at the air where Rose had been. She looked up at Rose, her eyes dark, her lips puffy, and her chest heaving. "What's wrong?"

"I'm not doing this. You have to choose." Rose barely managed a whisper as she backed away.

"What...I...Rose...please..." Alma's face contorted with confusion.

To keep herself from returning to Alma's outstretched arms, Rose had grabbed her bath towel from the drying rack by the door and run. The cold shower had done very little to calm the fire building inside, but it was all she had.

Until tonight. Once more her lips were on Alma's, their bodies flush together, and she was pretty sure everything she wished for was about to be granted. She let the kiss linger just long enough to make her heart beat a little faster and her breath come a little harder, then she pulled back. She didn't release her hold on Alma's waist and waited for Alma to meet her gaze.

Alma's lashes fluttered for a moment, then she looked at Rose with the darkest, most wanton, expression. Rose could fall into those eyes and never surface again. Alma stretched upward to bring her lips to Rose's again and Rose surrendered to the kiss for a moment. If this didn't answer her questions, nothing Alma said would quiet her doubts. Still, she ended the kiss before Alma was ready. She needed to hear the words.

"What's wrong?" Alma dropped her head against Rose's shoulder and struggled to catch her breath. She pressed herself tighter against Rose until Rose could feel Alma's heart beating hard inside her chest.

Gently, Rose eased away from Alma so they were able to

look at one another. "What do you want?"

"What...what do I want?" Alma shook her head and reached for Rose, her hands grasping at Rose's face.

"I need to hear you say it, Alma." Rose remained steadfast. God she wanted to give in, but it would hurt too much if she were wrong. Alma had the power to break her completely and this was her only chance of survival.

"You...God, Rose, I want *you*." Her voice trembled, dropping to an intimate whisper.

Rose pulled Alma close again. The separation between them, distance that didn't need to be there, was too much to bear. "Are you sure? After this, I won't share."

A loud burst of applause interrupted the moment and Alma glanced nervously at the door again. She licked her lips and then met Rose's gaze. Very carefully and deliberately, Alma nodded. "I'm sure." This time when she twined her fingers in Rose's hair and tugged, Rose went willingly into the kiss.

This wasn't the right place, not here with cheers and whistles breaking through the fragile tension of the moment. Not with the possibility of discovery and all the consequences that went with it. Not with the smell of bleach from the dishes battling for dominance over the ammonia they used to clean the floor. Rose had a permanent sheen to her hair from the grease they used to cook everything that wasn't steamed, and her nostrils were filled with an awful blend of cigarettes and half rotten potatoes.

But there was no right place in this God forsaken war. All they ever had was right here, right now. Everything else could be taken away in a moment.

None of the reasons to wait kept Rose from pushing Alma against the nearest set of shelves and prising Alma's mouth open with her tongue. Alma whimpered, the sweetest, softest sound that seared itself into Rose's memory. "God, you feel so good."

Alma gasped. "More...I want..."

Rose slanted her mouth over Alma's, muffling her plea as she teased Alma's tongue with her own. Slowly, she worked Alma's shirt free from her pants. She needed skin, just the tiniest gap between the layers of fabric. Then, miraculously, her finger grazed Alma's side. She eased her hand beneath Alma's thick uniform top, the fabric rough compared to the smooth, trembling silk of Alma's skin. She set her palm flush against Alma's side, spreading her fingers wide to take in as much as possible.

The heat beneath her touch took Rose by surprise. Despite the humidity and the temperatures, Alma always looked so cool, so put together, yet Rose's hand on her body brought a fire to her skin that the weather couldn't. It was a heady realization and Rose desperately wanted to feel *more*. She tugged at the fabric ineffectually and groaned. Alma was wearing way too many clothes. Her fingers shook as she worked the first button free from Alma's shirt. "Is this okay?"

God, she needed Alma to say yes. It would be cruel to be this turned on only to be turned down.

Alma nodded, and kissed Rose again. Her lips were intoxicating, overwhelming, and Alma's tongue sliding into her mouth stole her breath. She couldn't think. Alma unbuttoned the next several buttons for Rose, her hands making jerky, imprecise movements and she stopped completely when she reached the top button. Alma drew in a deep breath and gazed at Rose. She looked so vulnerable, and Rose felt guilty for pushing further than Alma was ready to go. She placed her hands over the top of Alma's to prevent her from undoing the last button.

"We don't have to..." Rose whispered and her voice trailed off completely at the end.

Alma kissed her carefully, a quick, precise meeting of their lips that showed no hesitation, only confident assurance. Then she looked at Rose, this time a little more certain, and she moved her fingers beneath Rose's to free the last button. "I want to." Alma's voice was steady and clear.

"Thank God." Rose brushed the shirt off Alma's shoulders and let it fall to the floor. She placed an easy kiss on Alma's neck, then another on her chest, at the top of the swell of her breast. Alma moaned and clutched Rose's head to her chest.

Rose was stuck in limbo between wanting to go painfully slow to draw out the pleasure for Alma, and wanting to fulfill her own desire *now* because she'd denied it for too long already. Instead of deciding, she simply let Alma's body speak to hers. The hitch in Alma's breath told her to suck a little harder on the swell of skin she had caught between her lips. The groan and the way she thrust her hips told Rose to slip her fingers beneath Alma's bra strap.

She closed her eyes and let herself enjoy the feel of Alma's body trembling beneath her touch when she eased her fingers along the line of fabric before drawing the strap down. As she peeled away the cup of her bra, Alma tightened the grip on her head, the pull of her hair causing pinpricks of pain over Rose's scalp. She released Alma's skin from her mouth with a pop, and moaned as she took Alma's nipple between her lips.

"Oh..." Alma's body drew tight and she held perfectly still. "Don't...good...please."

How was she supposed to go slow when Alma made sounds like that? Sounds that drew all the moisture in Rose's body to her pussy, and chased every thought from her mind save one—make Alma do that again. She wanted to hear Alma pant and moan and whisper incoherent commands. She wanted to hear her own name fall from Alma's lips when she found release.

All she could do, the only clear option available, was to lower the zipper on Alma's skirt. The click, snick, purr of the teeth as she eased the tab lower and lower echoed through the kitchen, too loud to ignore. She released Alma's nipple, flicked her tongue over it one more time just to hear Alma gasp, then asked, "Is this okay?"

Rose dipped her fingers beneath the loose fabric at Alma's waist to make sure she knew exactly what Rose was asking. They were very close to a point of no return. Some things simply can't be taken back.

Alma stared at her, eyes wide and filled with a lusty glaze. She nodded and drew Rose to her for another desperate, searching kiss.

"Are...you...sure?" Rose asked between kisses. God, she didn't want to stop and would crumble if Alma changed her mind at this point. But the risks were great and Alma deserved every opportunity to consider what she was asking, to withdraw to safer ground.

"Yes, please, Rose." Alma's answer was urgent, maybe even a little afraid, as if she thought Rose was going to stop. "Make me...I want...God." Alma grunted and attacked Rose's lips again. She moved with such burning need that part of Rose wanted to bring her to orgasm right that moment, then build her up again when everything wasn't so sharp between them.

But she couldn't. Not yet. She eased away enough to ask one last question. "Have you ever...you know?"

With anyone else, Rose wouldn't have asked. Or if she had, she would have simply asked if she'd fucked before. No fuss, no muss. Everything was so much simpler before Alma. But not nearly as sweet.

"No." Alma shook her head. "I mean yes. I have. Just not...you're the first..."

"Woman?" Rose finished for her, more to feed the swell of pride in her chest than to take away Alma's discomfort. The women in Alma's hometown we're obviously insane. Why else wouldn't they at least try?

Alma nodded, her gaze averted. Rose placed two fingers beneath Alma's chin and tipped her head back, urging Alma to look at her. Finally, Alma did, and her face blazed deep pink. Rose kissed her gently on the cheek just to taste the heat against her lips. Alma didn't look so embarrassed after that.

Rose opened her mouth to speak, but hesitated. "I..." She swallowed. She didn't have the words to express how happy Alma made her, how proud and pleased she was to be the first to share this with her, how honored she was for Alma to trust her with something so special. "I'll take care of you." It wasn't exactly what she wanted to say, but it was close enough.

"I trust you." Alma's voice was clear, and she spoke without hesitation. She cupped her hand around Rose's cheek and said it again, much softer, "I trust you." She held Rose's gaze and a shiver ran through Rose at the heavy meaning Alma infused into three small words.

She placed her own hand over Alma's and turned to press a kiss against Alma's palm. "Thank you," she whispered.

Alma ran her hands over Rose's arms, her movements tentative, but the look in her eyes determined. She reversed her movement, but instead of travelling up Rose's arm, she adjusted until her fingers trailed over Rose's abdomen. She stopped short, just below Rose's breasts. Rose drew in a sharp breath and waited. God, she could almost feel Alma's touch. She'd imagined it so many times and was overwhelmed to be here, now, in this moment. Alma stared into her eyes and, with deliberate care, raised her hands to cover Rose's breasts.

Rose didn't move, she stood as still as she could and let Alma have her way. For the longest moment, Alma left her hands resting there, immobile and with only the slightest pressure. Rose's breath grew ragged, shallow, and all she could focus on was the almost there touch of Alma's palms against her nipples. Her body strained to move closer, but she held herself back. This was about Alma, not about the ridiculous pounding heat shooting through Rose, starting deep down inside and pulsing outward. And when Alma finally moved, kneading Rose's breasts in her grip, Rose's vision swam and grew dim at the edges. She groaned in a way she wasn't used to hearing, and pushed herself farther into Alma's palm.

Alma studied her face, watching Rose react as she stroked and massaged and eventually pinched Rose's ability to speak, her ability to think, completely out of her head.

"God, that's amazing," Alma said, her voice filled with wonder.

Rose nodded because some response was needed, but speech wasn't an option. She nodded and forgot to stop when Alma rolled her nipples between her thumbs and forefingers. Even through the fabric of her uniform top and her bra, Alma's touch was sharp and brought another deep moan from somewhere inside Rose.

Alma eyes sparked with something between curiosity and excitement and she unbuttoned Rose's shirt with steady, sure fingers. In moments, Rose stood naked from the waist up, her shirt and bra on the floor at their feet. Alma descended without warning. One moment, she was staring with open fascination at Rose's breasts, the next she was sucking one deep into her mouth. She didn't hesitate, didn't build up. She pulled hard and didn't stop and Rose came embarrassingly close to orgasm just from the jolt of sensation.

Somewhere between kissing Alma and now, Rose had lost

the script. She'd promised to take care of Alma, but instead, she was a whimpering mess on the verge of pleading for release. It wouldn't take much, a well placed thigh, a few strokes from one finger. Hell, she was so close that the right look from Alma would break her into pieces. Control. She needed to regain control.

"Wait." Rose didn't recognize her voice. It came out as strangled growling moan with a "t" at the end. She pulled away just a fraction, trying to escape the relentless wave flowing from Alma's mouth directly to her clit via her nipple. Alma followed with a whimper and tightened her hold on Rose's hips, her fingers digging in and demanding that Rose stay right there and take it. Rose cleared her throat and tried to focus on un-sexy, non-orgasmic things. "Alma... Baby, wait, please."

She grasped helplessly at Alma, her hips rolling all on their own. Her whole body was betraying her and she was so far beyond regaining control. And then, as she was pulling tight and on the verge of cresting, Alma released her. Alma rose up and met her gaze. Her pupils were blown wide, face flushed, and she sucked in a deep, raspy breath. "Hmm?"

"L-let me..." Rose gave up trying to speak and let her hands explain what her words couldn't. She stared into Alma's eyes as she slowly reached around to unhook her bra. Alma helped her remove it, then guided Rose's hands to her skirt. Rose pushed the fabric down over the swell of Alma's hips and hooked her fingers in the elastic of her panties to send them to the floor at the same time. Alma gasped sharply as Rose dropped to her knees. She kissed Alma lightly on the stomach, just below her navel, and then helped her stepped out of the fabric pooled at her feet. Combat boots were good for a lot of things, but made removing panties a challenge.

Because she could, Rose brought her hands up the outside of Alma's legs. She moved slowly, mesmerized by the rise of goose bumps on Alma's soft skin. Rose tipped her head back to watch Alma's reaction as she eased her hands around her hips to settle on the swell of her backside. Alma's breath hitched when Rose squeezed the soft, pliant flesh, so Rose did it again. After one more kiss to Alma's belly, she forced herself to stand. It went against every lustful instinct urging her to bury her tongue in the moisture between Alma's thighs, but as much as she wanted to taste her, she wanted to watch Alma's face even more. They only got one first time, and she wanted every second etched forever in her memory.

Rose kissed Alma softly on the lips. She needed the brief moment of reconnection, but didn't want to get lost in it this time. The crowd gathered in the amphitheater outside burst into a sudden, loud roar of applause. The show was almost over and that meant they needed to hurry. Rose groaned. She didn't want the army to dictate the schedule on this moment as they did every other aspect of her life.

She took Alma's hands in hers and guided her to the stainless steel prep table. It wasn't ideal, but it was sturdy and flat and infinitely cleaner than the floor. She helped Alma climb up before joining her. The table was cool and hard and so far away from the soft mattress and candlelight that Alma deserved. As soon as they got back to the states, Rose would take her to the best hotel in the city and do this again the right way.

"You're so beautiful." She brushed her lips over Alma's as she eased her onto her back. It felt wrong to finally be here, in this moment, and still have her trousers on, but there wasn't time. This was supposed to be about Alma and she'd let herself get too distracted earlier. She gazed at Alma, affording the time to drink her in. From pebbled tips of her breasts—just enough to fill Rose's hand—to the slight swell of her belly, all the way to her manicured toes, Alma was exquisite.

"Rose..." Alma reached for her, her touch greedy and demanding as she pulled Rose down. She kissed Rose, a fiery opposite of what Rose had expected. Their bodies met, heated and flushed, as Alma arched against her and Rose groaned into her mouth. Alma whispered, "Please."

"Yes." Rose gripped Alma's waist, giving herself a moment to feel before she eased her hand lower. She traced the sharp edge of Alma's hipbone, letting it draw her hand closer to her destination. Alma shifted her body, parting her legs. As she had earlier announced her intention to kiss Alma, she said, "I'm going to touch you now. Okay?"

Alma swallowed hard and nodded, her hips lifting slightly. She squeezed Rose's shoulders and stared into her eyes. Yes, it was much better to watch Alma as she slid her fingers lower and lower until she finally dipped between Alma's legs. She urged Alma to spread her legs wider and straddled Alma's thigh. She settled her weight against Alma and all of her awareness shot to that perfect spot where her inseam pressed hard against her clit. She drew in a shaky breath and refocused on Alma. As long as she held herself rigid, she'd be okay. Any movement, and she would come first and that was not acceptable.

"Ready?" Rose asked the question at the same time as she parted Alma's lips and ran her fingers through her arousal. "So wet..."

Alma gasped, her grip on Rose's arms tightened to the point of pain and Rose knew she'd probably be bruised the next day. It was worth it. Alma whispered, "Don't stop."

"Never," she promised as she slid one finger inside Alma. She was so tight and the walls fluttered around Rose. She'd wait to fuck her like this another time, after her body got used to being loved. Rose withdrew and brought her finger to her mouth. Just a taste, that's all she needed. Alma watched as she licked her finger clean, then tugged her down into a hot, open-mouthed kiss. Alma licked inside her mouth and her moan vibrated against Rose's tongue.

Lost in the heady taste of Alma's wetness and her greedy kiss, Rose stopped trying to make it perfect. She touched Alma's clit, flicking over it and drawing it out. Alma was already rigid and swollen and Rose knew it wouldn't take much. She circled her fingers easily, and thrust against Alma's leg at the same time. If she timed it right, they would come together and Rose couldn't imagine anything more perfect.

A few frantic thrusts as she stroked Alma brought Rose to the edge hard and fast. Alma trembled beneath her, her body arching. She gasped and moaned. "Rose. God...yes..."

"Yes, just like that." Rose watched, enraptured, as Alma froze, her body extended and rigid, the slight sheen of sweat coating her body. She slowed her touch, easing Alma up and over the brink. She wanted to capture this moment, to hold it in her memory and compare it to every orgasm in Alma's future. She brushed a kiss over Alma's nipple, unable to resist the temptation of Alma's flesh as her body heaved in the last throes of her orgasm.

As Alma shuddered and descended from her peak, Rose surrendered to her own orgasm. Alma's name tumbled from her lips as her insides shattered. She thrust against Alma's thigh again and again, coaxing her release to last just a little longer.

Rose gathered Alma to her. Everything about this war, the blood and destruction and hate, was hell, and yet she'd found Alma. She held Alma, a final moment of perfection before they returned to the melee that surrounded them. The USO show was ending and the longer they stayed, the more likely their discovery. With a sigh, she untangled herself from Alma. She pressed one last kiss into Alma's hair and silently promised to take care of her, to see her through this war and safely home.

WATCHING

BY C.B. POTTS

1952: Korean War: South Korea

Erin was always watching, and it was driving me crazy.

I'd feel her gaze on me at the strangest times; first thing in the morning, when those of us not actively on duty would assemble loosely and watch for choppers or other less desirable incoming aircraft, I was the object of her attention while everyone else watched the skies. Her regard felt like an embrace; it had a hot, intimate weight all its own that lingered on my face. On my body.

When the casualties came in, of course, Erin was all business. She focused on her patients with a powerful intensity that marked her as an experienced OR nurse—that's what she had been doing, back home in Boston before the war, or so the scuttlebutt went. Our surgeons loved working with her because she seemed to know, almost intuitively, what they wanted before they even knew they wanted it. She was just always on—except when she was off. During the occasional merciful lull we'd enjoy in the operating theater, her brown eyes would meet mine, searching.

Searching for what, though, I didn't know. Outside of professional conversation, we never actually spoke. More than once we'd almost collided in the mess hall; finding ourselves abruptly face to face, practically touching, inches apart, we were strangely silent. Language abandoned us, and we were reduced to polite smiles and gestures, each insisting that the other go ahead.

Erin had no problem talking with other people. I'll admit to my own fair share of watching; I liked to see her joke around. She'd constantly be in the heart of the most active conversations, doing her part to keep the group's morale up. Everyone around her would be laughing, and Erin laughed loudest of them all. When she did, her short brown curls shook, and I'd find myself possessed by the need to touch them; I wanted to discover if they felt as silky as they looked. And there was such a light in her eyes. Erin had dimples in her cheeks when she smiled; the one in her right cheek was deeper and more pronounced than in her left.

We all lost weight in Korea, but you couldn't tell that from looking at Erin. She filled out her uniform beautifully; if I let myself think about it, it was easy to imagine how it would feel to cup her round breasts in my hands. Her hips were slim but swelled just enough that watching her walk away was both a torture and a delight. I couldn't help but look at her, but I was also a coward; when she caught me looking, I'd pretend I was looking elsewhere—toward the sky, or down at the muddy ruts we pretended were pathways, anywhere but where I'd been looking.

Nights were the best time to watch Erin. We were in the same barracks; our bunks were kitty corner to each other across the aisle. We weren't always on the same rotation—she worked a lot of days and I pulled more than my fair share of nights—but when we did bunk down at the same time, I definitely took advantage of the opportunity to check out her slender form while she slept. Every now and then I could feel her doing the same thing to me—or at least I thought I did.

And when the moon was full—or perhaps it was the way the stars lined themselves up— Erin and I would both be awake and watching each other in the small, still hours of the night. It would be bright enough to see the gleam in her eyes and the curve of her smile, but I couldn't tell if her hands were really moving beneath the thin blankets the way I'd hoped they were. The way my own hands moved.

Things might have gone on this way for eternity, or the remainder of war, whichever was longer, but then one morning our charge nurse, Captain Hyatt, announced the entire MASH unit was pulling up stakes to move sixty miles closer to the front.

If there's ever a good time to move a military hospital, this was it. We'd a relatively low patient count, and the jangma rains, which had been coming down non-stop for weeks, had stopped for almost thirty hours. But don't let those facts fool you. Nothing's ever simple in the Army. It'd be against regulations for things to run smoothly. Not all of our patients were going to be able to recover from their injuries in the field; they'd be journeying via helicopter to Navy vessels stationed off shore and from there to hospitals in Germany or even, if they were lucky, stateside.

"We're going to need two of you to stay back here with the corpsmen until the choppers make it in here for Wilson, Terrents and Franklin," Hyatt said, reading from her clipboard. She raised her gaze and looked at the handful of us; all tired from preparing the patients who'd been deemed healthy enough to move, all at least ten years younger than she herself was. "Do I have any volunteers?"

I swallowed and glanced toward Erin. For once, she wasn't looking at me. But what the hell, I thought, this might be my only chance to find out what she's been thinking. I raised my hand. "I'll do it."

Hyatt nodded, and a heartbeat passed. Then another, and I started thinking I was the world's biggest fool. A third heartbeat had me fully convinced, and I could see that Hyatt was about to choose someone. Then Erin coughed, stepped forward, and said, "Me too, Ma'am. I'll stay."

"You two should be all right," Hyatt said. "They wouldn't be moving us forward if this area wasn't secure. Still, keep your eyes open and your heads about you." She shook her head and waved the remaining trio of nurses toward the transport. They left us without a backward glance. Before Hyatt followed them, she turned and looked me in the eyes. "The minute those birds take off, I want you two in a jeep on your way forward. You got it?"

"Yes, Ma'am."

"Good nurses are hard to come by out here. I can't afford to lose either one of you." She pinched the bridge of her nose.

"Not with what's coming." It was Erin's turn to be held in Hyatt's regard. She held our Charge's gaze steadily, brown eyes unblinking. "Understood?"

"Yes, Ma'am." Erin smiled, and she reached forward and patted Hyatt on the shoulder. "It's okay, love. We'll be as careful as we can be." She tipped her head toward me and said, "This one still owes me $5. I can't let anything happen to her until I get that money back."

Hyatt laughed. It was like watching her shed an eighty pound pack; her shoulders leveled off and more air made its way into her lungs. "Well, in that case, I'll be going. See you soon, ladies."

"We'll see you soon, Ma'am."

Between the action at the front and the jangma rains, which of course started back up the moment the last of the 2069's trucks rolled out of sight, it was going to be hours before a chopper pilot would even think about bringing his bird our way. The odds were better than good we wouldn't see anyone before dawn. The corpsmen were pulling double-duty, theoretically patrolling a loose perimeter around the tent where our three casualties awaited pickup; in actuality keeping watch from wherever they could manage to stay dry.

"Well, this is going to be fun," Erin said. She'd just finished checking Terrent's vitals; there was so much morphine in that poor bastard's system it was amazing he had any vitals to check. Franklin was out like a light. Wilson's face was bandaged so heavily that we couldn't tell whether he was awake or not, but he was quiet and that was good enough. "You want to tell me why you volunteered us for this?"

I nodded toward the front of the tent, where a canvas wall portioned the supply storage area from the patients. "Let's talk in there."

"These guys can't hear you," she snorted.

"They left a bed up there," I blurted, and then, red-faced, stammered, "I mean, we can at least sit down. My feet are killing me."

Erin smiled. "By all means, let's go… talk."

At this time of year, the night came late in Korea, but when it arrived, it came fast. Without the rest of the 2069 around, our little tent was an isolated island in a sea of blackness. Op spec dictated keeping lighting minimal; we didn't want to attract more attention than the corpsmen could realistically handle. The supply room was dim at best. It was a good thing we didn't have to see far.

Erin and I were standing, face to face, belly to belly. You know how they tell dancing couples to always leave enough room for the Holy Ghost between them? That spirit was going to need to find some other couple to tango with; we had no space for him at all.

"So?" Erin said. Her eyes looked black, and her smile was white. "What do we have going on here, Dorie?"

"You've been looking, heavy," I said. "And I've been looking back."

"Heavy," she agreed. "I've noticed."

"So I thought I'd see what we were going to do about that," I said, and then lost my nerve. With girls, it's never a sure thing. I could have read this entire situation completely wrong. "I mean, if you want to."

Erin stepped closer. "I am so scared to touch you," she said, lips inches from mine, "because once I start, I'm not going to be able to stop."

The wind howled, and the tent shook around us. You didn't have to strain to hear the artillery in the distance; the shelling slowed down during the long Korean night, but it never actually stopped. Erin's hair did feel like silk when I slid my fingers into it. She didn't fight me as I pulled her closer. "I'm not one bit worried about that."

I'd thought I'd known something about kissing pretty girls. Erin taught me different. The first contact with her lips stopped my heart; her tongue gliding over mine brought it racing back to life. She tasted like fire, black coffee and gari—we were all eating the pickled ginger by then, it helped you forget how hungry you were—and I wanted more and more from her, kissing her as much as I'd ever known how to kiss.

She pulled her head back first and whispered "Wow". Then

she smiled, a smile I'd never seen before, and all of Korea disappeared. It was gone, every bit of it—the never ending jangma rains, the stupid buzzing flies, the heat, the cold, the fear, the casualties in the next room and the corpsmen outside, the constant shelling and the stupid, stupid war, all vanished, replaced entirely by the look on Erin's face.

"Wow," I agreed. I reached for her, and she reached for me. Erin's touch was lightning. Everywhere her finger tips brushed, I was burned. I was being incinerated, from the inside out.

"Wish we had more light," she said, pulling open my uniform buttons. Underneath mine, I'd had on a white tee shirt and the regulation bra; Erin, it turned out, was wearing nothing. "I want to see you."

There was thunder, there was lightning. For a flash, Erin had her wish. I saw that she was thinner than I'd imagined; beneath the swell of her breasts, I could spy the outline of her ribs. She was smaller out of uniform, but so much more approachable. It was easier to put my hands on her than it had ever been to talk with her.

"You're such a pretty thing," she said. Erin would touch and then kiss the same spot. Her knowing fingers traced and twisted round my nipples; followed fast by her tongue and the lightest brush of her teeth. It's a good thing we were sitting, because I would have fallen over when she did that – who knew a dirty kiss could feel so good?

We were sitting on the bed, and then we were laying on it, side by side at first, and then with her rolled up on top of me. Her belt came open easy enough. It took some pushing to get her pants off – I might have been better at it if she wasn't tugging at my pants at the same time – but after a few awkward moments we managed, and then we were tangled together, thighs scissored between each other's legs, grinding hard and kissing as much as we could between gasps and groans.

All at once, Erin reared up, biting her lip as she pushed down hard against me. Her entire body shook violently; I held onto her hips tight to keep her from pitching over out of the bed. She growled and twisted and became, for one brilliant moment, something other than the woman I'd been watching for so long; something I'd never even known to imagine. It took my breath away.

It was then we heard two sounds: the unmistakable thud-thud-thud of a chopper coming in and the corpsmen cursing up a storm as they ran for landing lights.

"You have got to be kidding me," Erin said. "Of all the times..."

"Here are your pants," I said, thrusting them toward her. "We've got to hurry."

"I know we've got to hurry," she snapped. She tossed my t-shirt at me. "I don't want to have to explain anything about this to Hyatt." There was something in her tone that made me suddenly question her relationship with our charge nurse, but this wasn't the time for that. I couldn't find my bra in the darkness, but this wasn't the time to worry about that mystery either. The minute my boots were on, I ran for the patients.

We'd agreed that we were going to move Franklin out first; he was the largest of our casualties which meant he needed to be positioned as close to the center of the craft as possible to keep the bird balanced. Erin had his feet and I'd just pulled the bag at his head when Svenson, one of our corpsmen, burst in with bad news. The chopper wasn't here to pick up our wounded. They had casualties they wanted to drop off.

"No one told them we've moved on," he shouted.

"They've got to go on up the road," Erin shouted back. "We can't help them here."

"They're telling me their guy won't make it that far," Svenson shouted. "He's going to bleed out before they get there."

"We've got no doctors!" I shouted at him.

"They've already dropped him," Svenson shouted. "And they're leaving right now." He was very loud. A moment ago we'd barely been able to hear him, but now his words echoed in the tent. The chopper had clearly departed.

"Son of a bitch!" Erin snarled. "You'd better bring him in, then. If he's going to die, I don't want him to die out in the rain."

"Yes, Ma'am," Svenson said, running for the door.

Erin looked at me. "What'd they leave us with?"

"Not a hell of a lot," I said. All of the surgery carts were gone; we'd been left with a minimal amount of dressings and painkillers to keep our patients stable until the evac choppers arrived. There was a tray with a couple of clamps and a suture kit, not nearly enough to handle anything serious.

And what we were facing was clearly serious. The corpsmen we worked with were a bunch of tough sons of bitches. They'd seen everything there was to see through the course of this stinking war: little farm boys blown almost in half, men missing limbs, what a brain pan looks like from the inside. But our new arrival made them pale-faced as they carried the stretcher in.

"Oh, Mother Mary, help me now," Erin said. She looked at me across the bed. "I don't even know what we can do about this." There was a young man in front of us with what had to be nine inches of jagged shrapnel embedded in the upper left quadrant of his chest; it was much nearer his heart than his shoulder. The field medics had packed it as best as they could, but blood was oozing from the wound steadily, a fresh surge appearing with every heartbeat.

"Do you think it's in his heart?" I asked her.

The passionate woman I'd held moments before was gone; she'd been replaced by an intensely focused clinician. "I don't think so," Erin replied. "If it was, he'd never have survived the flight. But it's damn near. Maybe he's nicked the pericarditis."

The patient groaned. His hands fluttered up toward the shrapnel. "Hold him, Dorie," Erin snapped. "I don't need him pulling on that damn thing."

I did as she asked, just as the kid groaned again. "Hurts...hurts so bad..."

"I know, honey. We're going to take care of it. You just need to lay still." I looked up at Erin. She already had a syringe in her hand. "You'd better hit him with that, because I don't think I'm going to be able to hold him."

She did, but morphine never works as fast as you need it to. The pain was clearly breaking through; it took all my strength to keep him down on the bed. Normally you lay across a patient in this situation, but you can't exactly do that when there's a huge shard of metal embedded in his chest.

"I'm going to have to try and get that out of there," Erin said. She shouted for Svenson, and had him take my place keeping the patient down.

"Erin," I said. "You don't know what you're dealing with." Pulling the shard out could easily prove fatal, and an intervention of this kind was definitely outside of our accepted scope of practice. "If it goes bad, he could die." I shook my head. "They'll pull your license. Send you home."

"You say that like it's a bad thing," she said. "And he's definitely going to die if we don't do it. Do we know when that damn evac chopper's coming in?" She glanced at Svenson; he shook his head. "So that's settled."

We prepped as best we could. The suture kit we had was adequate for a decent size wound, but we were well past that point. Erin muttered a string of prayers, Svenson wished her luck, and then, with a wad of dressing at the ready, Erin pulled the shrapnel out of the kid's shoulder.

It wasn't quite as long as we had feared, but it was jagged, with multiple sharp points. "Damn," Erin said. She'd covered the wound with dressing. It didn't turn crimson quite as fast as I'd expected, but there was definitely a good amount of blood. "I think it missed the heart, but I'll bet he at least nicked an artery. Clamp."

I handed her the clamp, and she pulled back the dressing. Speed is of the essence when working a chest wound; Erin moved rapidly but confidently to contain the bleeding. "I'm not going to be able to fix everything with what we've got."

"Arterial vessels first," I reminded her. The kid's vitals weren't great. "I'm losing pressure here; who knows how much blood he's lost already?"

"Too damn much." Erin was stitching quickly; it was easy to see why the surgeons left her to close so often. "I'd give anything for some suction."

All the pumps had gone to the front; Svenson and I looked at each other and then around the bare bones facility we'd been left with. We both saw the tourniquet tubing at the same time. "You don't think that'll work?" he asked.

"Make it work," Erin replied. "I can't see shit in here."

Siphoning blood from a wound isn't quite the same as liberating gas from someone else's tank, but it worked well enough to give Erin space enough to repair the worst of the damaged blood vessels before she ran out of suture. Svenson looked a little worse for wear after the experience, but war is like that.

"That's all we can do," Erin finally announced. "I can't do anything else for him." We packed the wound as best we could, wrapping yards of bandage around the boy to keep his shoulder still. "It's going to have to do until the chopper gets here."

I checked our patient's vitals again. His pressure had improved and his pulse had stabilized. "It's looking better than it was an hour ago."

"An hour?" Erin glanced toward the doorway. "It looks like the sun's coming up."

It was true; the horizon was turning that sickly yellow-green that signaled daybreak in Korea. I sighed, and suddenly felt the fact we'd not slept at all through every inch of my being. "At least the chopper should be here soon."

"Let's hope it's the right one," Erin said.

It didn't take long to find out; we heard the bird coming in just as we'd finished checking on our other three patients' conditions. None seemed the worse for going relatively unmonitored during our surprise surgery session; Terrents was fussy, but another hit of morphine resolved that. This time, luck was with us: the corpsmen ported our wounded out, and thankfully the chopper had the room to transport an additional casualty.

All that was left for us to do was drive the sixty mile route to reconnect with the 2069. We stood in the yard, looking at the jeep. Behind us, the corpsmen were emptying the scant contents of the med tent into the back of the transport tent. Soon, there'd be no sign there'd ever been a MASH unit here at all.

"We could always get lost," I suggested. "No one says we have to go back to the war." Korea stretched out all around us; there were a million wrong turns just waiting for us to take them.

"Nobody but Uncle Sam," Erin sighed. "And Hyatt would never forgive me if we bugged out on her."

I looked at Erin then. "Are you and Hyatt...like you and me?"

Erin laughed. "Baby, there's nobody like there's you and me. There's never been anyone like there's you and me."

I smiled then, surprised at how good her words felt in my ears. "So we should get going then?"

"I think we really should," Erin said, nodding toward the tent. One of the corpsmen was walking out with my bra in his hand. "Because I really don't want to hear anything he's got to say, do you?"

"Nope." I slid into the passenger seat, she took the driver's. "Not a word."

She hit the gas, and we were off. Only after we could no longer see the corpsman behind us, standing in the dust, holding lingerie and looking confused, did we let ourselves burst out laughing—and we laughed all the way until we rejoined MASH unit 2069.

DANGER

BY SACCHI GREEN

1969: Vietnam War: Greenwich Village, New York

Sex. Anonymous, no-strings, cunt-clenching, blast-furnace sex, enough to get me through a few more months of repression. That's all I was looking for. But deep down, it wasn't that simple. What I needed was danger, or pain, or pleasure; anything intense enough to fill the void.

Cruising Greenwich Village wouldn't block out flashbacks to Vietnam. Not a chance. But the war had cursed plenty of us with something besides nightmares and memory lapses and the whole PTSD bag. Only somebody who'd been there could understand the addiction, the need for adrenaline highs. Sometimes sex was the closest you could come. If you got really, really lucky, it might even make you forget for a while.

After a year at a field hospital at Pleiku in the boonies and six months at the main facility in Long Binh, I'd finally been rotated "home" and assigned to an Army orthopedic ward. It didn't feel like home. I didn't fit stateside any more, didn't fit anywhere, and over there the war still ground on into a future I wanted no part of.

There wasn't much of anything I did want, except enough of what passed for sanity to get me through my days. But I was needed; broken men who deserved far more depended on my care; and to keep from flaming out at my job I had to get away from it, if only briefly. So, on a rare weekend off, I took the train from DC to New York, and then the subway, rolling into the Christopher Street station at half-past midnight on June

28th, 1969.

Sweat, piss, and pot smoke soured the underground air. The street-level atmosphere was more breathable, but with an electric edge to it, a manic energy driving the crowds. I wasn't the only one looking for trouble. Local talent and weekend wannabes, hippies, hustlers, aging beatniks, tourists sucking up the scene; they wound in and out of bars and side streets along Sheridan Square. Mostly guys, but a few women of interest caught my attention as I edged through the throng.

The fringe on a leather jacket brushed my arm in the crosswalk. A sideways glance showed me a lean, tanned face framed by black hair, small feathers tucked into each long braid. A swift jolt of attraction—but my interest would fizzle if the body beneath the Indian regalia turned out to be male. I couldn't make up my mind until I'd dropped back far enough to watch her hips and long legs. Nice ass under the worn jeans, slim, but definitely female. Hippie role-play getups usually leave me cold; on the other hand, a nice touch of sexual ambiguity heats me up, so she'd scored at least a draw.

Once on the sidewalk, she turned and eyed me with more than the usual speculation, as if she thought she'd met me somewhere. Or was considering trying that line of approach.

I needed some decompression time. My gaze drifted past hers with only the subtlest pause at her slim, strong hands, as brown as her face. Maybe later, if she turned up at one of the bars I'd be checking out. I kept on toward my friend's apartment just off the Square on Grove Street, and felt the stranger watching me, felt my own stride alter subtly. My ass tingled. Then I heard her boots on the pavement as she moved away in another direction.

The leather-fetish shop just up the way was closed, but I took a look into its brightly lit windows anyway, reinforcing the sense that no, Dorothy, we weren't in Kansas any more, thank-you-very-much. Or in Washington DC at Walter Reed Army Hospital, although some of the S/M gear with its metal rivets and buckles gave me an unsettling flashback to the orthopedic ward.

I shook it off. Something different niggled at my mind as I dug out my keys and let myself in through the outer door.

Kansas, Dorothy...a headline glimpsed at the newsstand in Penn Station.... Oh, right. Judy Garland's funeral had been today. Maybe that explained the crowd's tension, maybe not. I hadn't been a huge fan, but still...I paused for breath on the fourth floor landing, and murmured sincerely, "Thank you, Dorothy, really, thank you very much." Then my key clicked in the old lock, and I went on in.

My college friend, off in Kenya now with the Peace Corps, still hung on to her rent-controlled apartment. I chipped in for occasional weekends. The anonymity of the city suited me, and the edginess of the Village. Not to mention the potential for sex, with all its dangers. Okay, especially with all its dangers.

By ten past one I was showered and ready to roll. Jeans and a denim vest over a gray T-shirt, auburn hair just brushing my earlobes. Not advertising, exactly, but not discouraging anybody who might be shopping.

Sheridan Square was boy-bar territory. I took a look around, though, the memory of the tall stranger percolating to the surface of my mind. The notion of slipping my hands under that fringed suede jacket took on considerable appeal. The thought of her fingers under my own shirt roused my nipples to parade-ground attention. Had I missed my chance?

The crowd was even edgier now. Some folks went about business as usual, whether strutting or furtive, while others clustered in muttering groups. I paused outside the Stonewall Inn. The usual go-go boys didn't interest me, although some of the drag queens could be as much fun to watch as high femmes, when I was in the mood.

But flashy drama wasn't on my wish list tonight. I needed the touch of smooth, unscarred skin, the press of an unbroken body needing no more healing from me than the frenzy of mutual friction could provide. I needed a woman.

No drama? So what the hell am I doing on the streets of Greenwich Village after midnight?

And there it came, like the answer to a subconscious prayer. Four black-and-whites and a paddy wagon squealed to a halt in front of the Stonewall Inn. Cops poured out like circus clowns, rushing to get an eyeful in the bar before the "degenerates" slipped out the back.

It was a regular routine. A flurry of arrests, a few fleeing customers who couldn't afford to be outed, some stiff fines, and then business as usual by the next night. But this time was different, and if you travel in the circles I do, or even if you don't, there's no need to explain the difference. Stonewall is in the history books.

My first instinct was to back off and head for more likely hunting grounds. Other folks seemed to have the same reaction, and the square was emptying fast. I walked a few blocks, going with the flow. But then the sirens of police reinforcements tore through the heavy air, and, instead of accelerating our retreat, turned the tide. Why did they need reinforcements? Something was happening. Something we didn't want to miss.

Back in the square screams and shouts and the crash of breaking furniture came from the Inn. A tangle of cops with billy clubs and drag queens wielding lethal spike heels came flailing out onto the sidewalk. The queers were fighting back!

And so, suddenly, was the crowd, scream by scream, stone by stone, chaos racing on a torrent of long-repressed rage.

I was near the front, with no thought but to ride the wave of excitement, until I saw her thirty feet away. Dark braids flailed like whips as four cops tried to drag her toward the paddy wagon. I stared, caught her eye, and for an instant she flashed me a cocky grin, the fire of battle flaring in her eyes. She wrenched one arm free long enough to give me a "thumbs up" sign. That brief glimpse of her hand hit me where it counted.

I swerved on impulse to charge to her aid, but a bottle shot past me from behind and exploded against a wall. War-zone reflexes slammed me to the pavement. When the crowd closed in it was move or be trampled, so I struggled upright and moved. By then there was no sign of her, and the cops were crouching behind their vehicle.

For an hour or so I hung around on the periphery of the action, not quite feeling like I had a right to be in the front lines. I'd never been hassled by the law, and in the military I'd kept a low, clean profile because my nursing was needed. Or so I told myself. Now I played medic to a few victims of shattered glass and pavement abrasions, applying disinfectants and band-aids from an all-night drugstore and ice packs rigged up in nearby bars. In between I cheered on the drag queens and pretty boys and bears of all flavors who turned the tables on the cops until the boys in blue had to barricade themselves inside the Stonewall Inn and call for more reinforcements.

Once in a while I caught distant glimpses of long black braids and a fringed jacket in the heart of the fight, where uprooted parking meters and benches were being used as battering rams to try to get at the police pinned down inside the tavern. She'd got loose, of course. Whenever I tried to get closer she disappeared into the shifting masses.

Frustration gnawed at me. All geared up, and nowhere to go. I'd come looking for sex, and the charged, manic atmosphere just pumped up my need, but this time groping in a secluded booth at a girls' bar wasn't going to do it for me. Even a wrestling match in a grubby restroom would be too tame. Even...

"Hey, medic, over here."

She was down a blind alleyway, slouching against a wall just at the blurred border where dim light gave way to darkness. Her fringed jacket was off, and slung over one shoulder.

Medic. She must have seen me patching up the wounded, but I hoped she wanted something more than first aid. Either way, I didn't hesitate for an instant. "Are you okay?" I didn't see any obvious signs of injury even when my vest brushed against her sweat-streaked tank top. "What do you need?"

No smile now, just a long, searching look into my eyes. My breathing quickened. So did my pulse rate, and an aching knot of need tightened my groin.

"What do *you* need, medic?" It wasn't a question. Her voice was low, husky, and certain. My answer was a half-step forward that brought me up firmly against her. One thigh pressed into her crotch. I straddled her slightly raised knee. Just a little more pressure, the slowest of movements...the need was building, along with the haunting fear of giving in to a need for more than I could get.

A glare of blue light flashed past the end of the alley as a cop car sped by. My back was exposed, vulnerable. What if I were caught, arrested, disgraced, fired...

The prickle of fear down my spine made my pulses beat even faster, my body strain harder to feel the responding pressure of hers. I clutched at her back, my hands already under her thin shirt, raising it. Her arms were around me, and she gripped my ass, forcing me to move, to rub against her in a rhythm that demanded fierce acceleration. "What do you need, what do you need," she muttered over and over, a low, compelling chant, and all I could do was move faster, rub harder, feel her hardened nipples flick across my aching breasts, and slide my cunt along her thigh while my own thigh met her thrusts.

Distant crashes...panic threatening to take hold...but she edged a hand inside my jeans and wrenched all my awareness back to where our bodies merged. Her fingers slid through my folds into my hungry cunt, her thumb went at my clit with hard, sure strokes—and I plummeted over the edge, all defenses gone, all trust given, nothing mattering but to get more, and more, harder, please, more!—until the whole battery of sensations, fear, urgent need, loss of control, came together in one massive jolt of pleasure.

It took a while to breathe again without panting. I knew I'd been dangerously noisy, and didn't care. She still held me close, without demand, although I could feel her heavy breathing.

It was my turn to chant, "What do you need, what do you need..." but my voice was muffled, first against her sweaty throat, then in the swell of her high breasts, then in the curve of waist and belly, and lower still. She was the one getting noisy now. By the time my knees ground into the alley's grit I had her zipper open and her briefs worked down enough to give my tongue and fingers access.

The intensity of her taste; the deep, rasping moans vibrating right through into my mouth; the flailing of long hair as her head thrashed back and forth—I wanted to savor all these, but I let the thrusting of her pelvis set the pace. The faster I licked and rubbed, the harder she needed it, until she came in such a flurry of violent jerks that I had to hold tight to stay with her. I managed to hang on, not easing up, until at last she pulled back and sank down beside me.

"So," she said between shuddering gasps, "you come here often, medic?"

"Never did an alley before," I said. "Always bars."

"And always strangers?"

"Always." I was still in too much of a post-fuck daze to think clearly.

She was quiet for a minute or two, catching her breath, maybe pondering in ways I was too dense to notice then. Finally she stood, giving me a hand to help me up. "Alright then. Glad I qualified. Thanks for the ride. Maybe I'll see you around." She moved out of the alley into the light of the city, and then she was gone, leaving me with a hazy feeling that however well I'd been fucked, I'd somehow really fucked up.

The action in the alley had drained me, but only for a while. The turmoil of protest was still roiling up and down one street or another, recharging me to a high pitch of nervous energy, so I went to check out the girl bars after all. No prospects that came close to what I needed. Not that I even knew what I needed any more.

When massive police forces with riot shields finally arrived, the battling crowds fragmented into pockets of guerilla action and then drifted away like tendrils of pot smoke. Anybody left on the streets was in danger of arrest, or worse. A remnant of survival instinct sent me hurrying toward the apartment.

"Hey...medic..." The voice was low this time, strained. She emerged from the shadows across the street, exhausted, bedraggled, shivering, coming down from the high of surging adrenaline. The hair straggling loose from one braid was sticky with blood. "Come on in," I said, and unlocked the door.

After three flights of stairs, her face looked greenish in the harsh light of the kitchen. "Sit down," I ordered. "Head between your knees." She obeyed without question, long, strong hands braced on her booted ankles. I thought wryly that having her head between my own knees would have been my first choice in other circumstances.

She'd caught a hit above her left ear hard enough to split the skin and raise a still-swelling lump. "Did you pass out when you got hit?" I was cleaning the wound gently with a soaking wet dishtowel. I'd already had a look at her eyes and didn't see any signs of concussion.

"Nope. Just got real mad. And maybe a tad destructive." Her voice was getting steadier.

"You're lucky to have such a thick skull." I felt around through her hair for more damage.

"Lucky to find a cute nurse close at hand." A cocky attitude isn't easy to pull off with your head down and bloody water trickling over your neck and down your chin, but she managed. There was something about the tone of voice, and an old, raised scar across the nape of her neck that diverted the flow of reddened water... I knew with sudden certainty that "Haven't we met somewhere?" wouldn't have been just a hackneyed pick-up line, after all. That scar was just about a year and a half old, the result of a mortar attack that blasted her ambulance apart and killed an already-wounded soldier. Her collarbone had been broken, too, but she'd managed to get the other two guys out and away before flames hit the gas tank.

I let her sit up while I went to fix an ice pack. "What makes you think I'm a nurse?" Stupid question. So much for anonymity. Not that she'd be likely to give me away to the Army bureaucracy, but some fear even deeper made my gut tense, some danger I couldn't even give a name.

"Well, you were one hell of a nurse in Long Binh, and I figure that's something you never forget. Like riding a bike. Or a woman." Her grin, now that I could see it, was cocky, too, but her eyes were grimly sober. She knew all about the things I couldn't forget. She'd been there, too, right through the worst of it. Her hair had been much shorter, not quite as dark, and the only time I'd seen her up close was when I was stitching up that gash on the nape of her neck. I might not have recognized anything about her, even my own handiwork—but I did remember the cockiness under stress. And those hands.

"You were in 'Nam, right? Ambulance driver?" I pressed the ice pack against her wound. "Hold that." Her hand went up obediently.

"Jeep jockey, mostly, on loan to the nurse's motor pool from the WAC base at Long Binh. When things got hot, every vehicle had to double as an ambulance."

I drew a deep breath. "And nurses had to be doctors half the time."

"Right." She held out the hand that wasn't holding the ice. "Thanks for the fine stitching job, Kim. I asked around about your name."

"You're more than welcome...Gale, isn't it?" I shook her hand, then forced myself to let it go. "Once we get the swelling under control, I'll put on a dressing, and you can hang out here tonight and get some rest."

Whether she had a concussion or not—could be a mild Class A—she had to be badly shaken, her defenses down. Better stick to the nurse role. "How about a bite to eat?" I went to the cupboard and riffled through it. "Hungry?"

"Could work up an appetite." Gale's tone made me glance back over my shoulder. She was surveying my ass and back with open appreciation.

"Definitely a sign of recovery." I put some chicken noodle soup on to heat. Not such weak defenses, after all, if her offensive game was anything to go by.

"A little something to keep your strength up," I told her, once I'd set out soup and crackers for us both and sat down at the table to join her. Then, while she was still formulating a snappy comeback, I turned seriously apologetic. "I'm sorry I didn't recognize you sooner. It was...hard, over there, keeping a balance between caring enough about patients and not caring too much. And afterward there was so much to block out..."

She started to shake her head, and winced. "No problem. I figure I got more mileage tonight out of being a stranger." The grin she managed was strained. My various sensitized pulse points stirred hopefully at the reminder, but I swung back into nurse mode with an effort, gathering up disinfectant and scissors and bandages from the bathroom.

"Yeah, well..." I felt my face flush. "Back to business for now. This will sting a little. And I'm going to have to snip some hair around the wound site."

"Hack it all off," Gale said curtly. "If I hit the streets

tomorrow looking anything like I did tonight, I'd be painting a bright red target on my ass. The cops are probably throwing darts at sketches of me right now"

I gave her a trim that, bandage aside, left her looking like the teen-aged love child of Katherine Hepburn and Marlon Brando. Elegant cheekbones, short, unruly hair, sultry eyes. "You clean up pretty well," I told her. "The image of a target on your ass is pretty intriguing, though. You sure there isn't one there already? Was all that..." I motioned toward the fringed jacket and the braided, dyed hair showing above the rim of the wicker wastebasket, "...some kind of disguise? You're not just worried about the local cops, are you."

An attempted shrug made her wince again. She yawned and rubbed her eyes, shock and exhaustion beginning to catch up to her, but she answered frankly. "I'm AWOL, and wanted by everybody from the MPs to the Oakland Police Department to the SDS. A little episode coming out of the Oakland Army Base just after I got stateside."

I knew all too well the treatment a uniform could get you back in the land of your birth. Even nurses ran the risk of taunts and spitting when protesters got their mob mentality on. I might agree with some of what they were for, but their methods seemed like the mindless tantrums of over-privileged brats.

"That bad, huh?" I wished I hadn't brought up the subject. She didn't need any more stress tonight.

"It wasn't what they yelled at *me*. I hadn't slept for forty-eight hours, had waking nightmares, barely remembered my own name, and I still kept my shit together through all that. But there was this guy in a wheelchair, a Marine. When they threw things, he couldn't get out of the way fast enough. I don't even remember much after that, but I know I grabbed a *Babykiller* sign and started swinging it. Some people got hurt. I ran, and kept on running."

Her head slumped. I caught it against my breast as my arms went around her. "Come on to bed now," I said, my lips brushing her hair so lightly she couldn't have felt them. So much for my longing for unscarred, unbroken women. What a delusion.

She managed to stand, moved across to the bedroom with my help, and even tried to pull me down beside her while I eased her clothes off. "Later," I said, and turned out the lights. "Get some sleep now. Nurse's orders."

A faint glow of sunrise already showed around the curtains. I sat and watched Gale sleep for a while, nearly dozing myself. I was wrung out, and hyped up, a combination not optimal for clear thought.

A trashcan lid clanged outside. A split second later an unearthly string of explosions rocked the air. Firecrackers, not grenades, I realized, after the first panicked lurch of my heart, but by then I was holding tight to Gale as she thrashed and kicked and yelled in short, incoherent bursts.

"It's all right," I said, soothingly and then more sharply, trying to penetrate her nightmare. "It's okay, all right, you're safe, I've got you." It took a while, and at least once her kicks knocked me off of the bed. "Cut it out!" I yelled at last, and then, as her eyes finally opened, I said, "It's me, Kim, the nurse, remember?"

She stared, still not quite awake. The kicking stopped, but shivering set in, in spite of the blankets I'd pulled over her. "It's all right," I repeated, pulling off my clothes. "You're safe, here, with me." I crawled under the covers to warm her and pressed my body along the length of hers. "Remember?"

"Medic," she muttered. "What..."

"Just firecrackers in a trash can. It's okay. We're safe." I held her closer, and she relaxed a little. "Remember last night?"

Now her arms went around me. Relaxation gave way to something entirely different. "Remember last night? Always." She moved against me, sliding her body along mine, and I responded in ways wholly unrelated to nursing ethics.

"Careful," I said, and rolled her gently on her back. "Don't move your head too much. Take it slowly, just let me...gently..." So she did, or tried, until the slow, achingly sweet movements of skin on skin, fingers stroking along curves and hollows and burrowing into deep warm places, mouths feasting on just about everything, led to rolling waves of pleasure that ultimately demanded a faster pace. Thrusts became harder, licks alternated with bites, until we were both sobbing in our desperate need—and then even harder in our release.

Gale slept again. I watched her face, vulnerable in this temporary illusion of safety, and faced my own vulnerability. Danger was a bond between us; the fear of it, the need of it, the inability to trust in peace. On some deep level, though, we did trust each other. That scared me right down to my bones. To open up, to let yourself care, was to offer a hostage to an ever-cruel fate.

She slept all day, and finally left as the protests were picking up steam again. "I have to move on, Kim. At least for now. Probably get into more trouble. I wish..."

"I know. I have to go back to work. People need me."

"I know all about needing you. If there are times—if I track you down..."

"I'll be there. No matter what, or when." I gave her an address that would always, eventually, reach me. And did, many times over the years, when she needed healing, or bail money, or sex with nothing held back; until finally it wasn't necessary any longer. The time came when we needed to be together even more than we needed danger, and by then there were places where the world had changed enough that we didn't have to hide from anything. Even ourselves.

Even though there was still, and always, war somewhere in the world.

ABOUT THE WRITERS

Jove Belle lives in the Pacific Northwest with her wife and children. She is the author of seven novels (*The Job, Uncommon Romance, Love and Devotion, Indelible, Chaps, Split the Aces, and Edge of Darkness*), all available from Bold Strokes Books. Learn more about Jove online at jovebelle.com.

Dena Hankins writes aboard her boat, wherever she has sailed it. After eight years as a sex educator, she started writing erotic tales with far-flung settings—India, North Carolina, deep space—and queer/trans romance novels. *Blue Water Dreams* struggles with magnetism and self-sufficiency while *Heart of the Lilikoi* explores colonization, environmentalism, and control over the future of Hawai'i amid sabotage, suspense, and heart-wrenching, searing hot sex.

J.B. Hickock, "John" to his friends, is a writer, Luddite, and budding supervillain who likes writing with pen and paper, can't understand Facebook, and divides his time between dealing with affectionate animals, writing, and plotting his inevitable conquest of the world.

Victoria Janssen has written three novels for Harlequin, including *The Duchess, Her Maid, The Groom and Their Lover,* as well as short stories. Her recent work may be found in *Morning, Noon and Night; The Mammoth Book of Best New Erotica 12*; and *Sudden Sex.* Find out more at victoriajanssen.com.

Cara Patterson is an Edinburgh-based Scottish writer. She has been telling stories since before she can remember, and progressed onto writing them down as soon as she had a grasp of the alphabet. She's delighted to be able to say she is now a published author.

Field nursing has long been a fascination for **CB Potts**, whether in the wilds of war-torn Korea or the battlefields of America's Civil War. A copywriter by day, CB splits the rest of her day between wrangling two amazing kids, fiction writing, and a garden that, if left unattended for a single second, threatens to take over the entire world. Read about her adventures at cbpotts.livejournal.com or on Twitter @CBPotts.

Pascal Scott is the pseudonym of a writer of short fiction and poetry whose work has appeared in many ezines and print publications including *Harrington Lesbian Literary Quarterly*, *Southern Gothic*, *Khimairal Ink*, and others. Originally from California, for the past seventeen years she has lived in the mountains of North Carolina. "War of the Rebellion" is her first step into the literary world of lesbian erotica.

Jessica Taylor (jessicataylorwriter.com) is hard at work on her first novel, an MMA erotic romance. You can read more of her erotica in *Spy Games: Thrilling Spy Erotica.* Her literary fiction can be found online at Section 8 Magazine and wordhaus. Jessica is the winner of a Texas Health Resources Literature and Medicine award and two Katey Lehman Awards for creative writing. She lives, writes, and fights out of Austin, Texas. If you follow her on twitter, @jessahtaylor, it would make her day.

Sacchi Green is a writer and editor of erotica and other stimulating genres, with the extra benefit of a thigh-high accumulation of contributor's copies with rather startling covers. Her passion for history is even greater than her passion for, well, passion, so she's profoundly grateful to publisher Steve Berman for the chance to combine history and erotica in this anthology for Lethe Press.

Her home is in western Massachusetts, with an alternate retreat in the mountains of New Hampshire. She does makes regular forays into the real world, but her farthest and wildest journeys are taken in her mind, and shared in her fiction.

Sacchi's stories have appeared in scores of publications,

including *Best Lesbian Erotica, Best Women's Erotica, Best Lesbian Romance, Best Transgender Erotica, Best Fantasy Erotica, Penthouse,* and a collection of her own work, *A Ride to Remember.* In recent years she's taken to wielding the editorial whip, editing or co-editing nine lesbian erotica anthologies, while her alter-ego Connie Wilkins has been writing and editing speculative fiction, including *Time Well Bent: Queer Alternative History* and *Heiresses of Russ 2012: the Year's Best Lesbian Speculative Fiction* (co-edited with Steve Berman.) Between them, Sacchi and Connie have produced seven Lambda Award Finalists, with two winners.

Sacchi can be found online at facebook.com/sacchi.green and at sacchi-green.blogspot.com.

CPSIA information can be obtained
at www.ICGtesting.com
Printed in the USA
FFOW03n2139141215
19366FF

9 781590 215920